Sleep Well

Tales from the Mind Field

A Collection of Short Stories

By
R.M.Villoria

$4⁰⁰
A&L
8/25 ∕

The Agent, by R.M. Villoria. Copyright © 1994.
Long Distance Love, by R.M. Villoria. Copyright © 2013.
Dead End, by R.M. Villoria. Copyright © 2013.
U.S. Library of Congress Cataloging
Shadows, by R.M. Villoria. Copyright © 1993 #577630.
Going Home, by R.M. Villoria. Copyright © 1993 #550920.

Acknowledgments

My thanks to Nicole Villoria whose assistance with editing has helped enormously and whose consistent support is greatly appreciated. To my wife whose patience and support has helped drive me to continue on.

CONTENTS

Tales from the Mind Field

SHADOWS
By
R.M.Villoria

Prologue

As the crow flies, you can reach it in forty-five minutes to an hour from Reno, but driving the winding mountain roads up to Glenridge Academy, nestled high in the Sierra Mountains, usually takes the better part of two hours. You know you're there when you come around Spirit Rock. So named for the old Indian legend regarding the ancestors of the original Native American dwellers that are buried around there. As you look down to your right about 600 feet below, you can see the little campus almost hidden amongst the pines. From here it still takes you a good fifteen minutes to descend down the narrow roadway and through the massive wrought iron gates to the main building. As you pull up in front, you can't help but stare for a moment at the enormity of this old brick structure. It was built back in the late 1800's by a group of Virginia City silver miners as a vault of sorts because of it's impenetrable walls.

Later abandoned, it and the grounds on which it stands were purchased by a wealthy Pennsylvania family with four daughters. Wanting only the best in education for his children, the patriarch of the family started an all girls academy and as it grew in size, it's reputation did as well. Soon well-heeled families from all over the country were sending their daughters here to the mountains for their education. It began as simply an elementary school, but as his daughters grew so did the academy, until it included high school and several more buildings. Dormitories were constructed to house the many out of the area students. For many years the Glenridge Academy came under pressure to become a co-ed institution, however the descendants of the original founder held fast to his desires that it remain an all-girls school. Finally in 1978, the board of directors were forced to put the growing requests to a vote.

Unanimously, Glenridge Academy became a co-educational institution and grew even greater in reputation and size. Every year or so it seemed that there was something new being added to the campus. Sports fields, a new building for laboratories and classrooms, tennis courts, the campus was a shining example of higher academe. And now in 1990, the main building, a rambling brick edifice over 100 years old was finally being restored to its original condition and listed among the states historical buildings. And with this milestone came an unimaginable horror no one could have ever imagined.

Chapter 1

```
┌──────────────────────────────────┐
│        GLENRIDGE ACADEMY         │
│          Presents it's           │
│              1990                │
│       SPRING FLING DANCE         │
│                                  │
│   Friday May 12th      6-10 pm   │
│        Academy Auditorium        │
└──────────────────────────────────┘
```

   Brenda Cummings, the schools administrative secretary, stared at the announcement. She really wasn't looking forward to chaperoning another one of these dance events again this year. Last year's spring dance had been pretty trying for her, dealing with a room full of rich kids with little respect and the alcohol…oh yes, she couldn't forget the alcohol. Why did she always volunteer for these things anyway she thought? She was about to place the card back in the box with the rest of the announcements that were to be distributed later that day, when suddenly the entire room shook with a tremendous jolt.

   "What the heck was that!" she said as she jumped up from her chair.

   It seemed to her as though a medium sized tremor had hit the campus. Having moved here from southern California, she knew only too well what an earthquake was. Several of the plaques on the wall were knocked off onto the floor and dust and spackling from the ceiling had settled on to her desk. Mr. Thompson, the academy's Chancellor, came out from his office. His six foot plus frame made a striking presence in the doorway. A direct descendant of the original founder, he took great pride in the academy. As Chancellor he oversaw every aspect of each days agenda as well as anything else that was going on around the campus. His pet project right now though was the work going on right outside his office window.

"Are we under siege?" he said jokingly as he and Brenda walked out into the hallway.

They were met by two of the construction crew that were working on the restoration of the building.

"I apologize sir," one of them said as they approached. "One of our men accidentally ran the back hoe into the side of the building. I hope we didn't scare you too much."

"No, I just hope you didn't do any real damage. That was a pretty good bump and this is a pretty old place," Thompson answered looking around the hallway and at the main entryway.

It had taken six years of convincing and plenty of red tape, but finally the old structure was going to be restored back to its original condition. This was a project Jack Thompson had wanted to see accomplished before he retired and finally it was going to happen. That was of course, if the men working on it didn't completely knock the old place down first.

"Just a few bricks knocked loose from up above sir, that's all."

"I'm glad I had my hard hat on," the other worker added smiling.

The two men turned and walked back outside.

As Brenda and her boss turned to re-enter the office, Jack stopped and looked up the massive wooden staircase that led to the second story and the attic beyond.

"Did you hear that?" he asked Brenda.

"What? I didn't hear anything," she replied.

Thompson shrugged his shoulders as though to discount the noise as nothing more than his imagination and walked back to his office.

Across campus, Suzy Jennings could have cared less about next months dance however. It was the event that would take place this Friday night that kept her anxiously counting the hours until the end of the week.

"You're crazy," her girlfriend said from across the cafeteria table. "What is this, the eighth or ninth guy you've gone to bed with this year? You almost got expelled the last time you got caught."

For Suzy, it was a sport and the more guys she could seduce the better she felt about herself.

"Don't worry, I won't get caught. Besides, I have my reputation to live up to don't I?" Suzy said sarcastically as she got up and walked out of the cafeteria.

Suzy's reputation did in fact precede her. It was more of a challenge than anything else to her. Since she had started here at Glenridge, she had been caught several times sneaking boys up to her dorm room or in other locations around campus where she would carry out her illicit trysts.

She had been threatened with expulsion on several occasions and had even had her parents called by Mr. Thompson to put them on notice. Yet, she was still here, now in her senior year and carrying on right to the end.

As she stepped out into the sunlight from the main building where the cafeteria was located, she glanced over at the workers off to the side of the steps. Suzy always tried to dress as suggestively as possible, her theory being that she never knew when an opportunity might arise that would pay off for her. Now she saw that she had caught the eye of one of the young men working on the restoration project. With his shirt off and the sweat glistening on his muscles, she immediately knew what she wanted to do. She walked over to the railing and looked down as if surveying the work that he was doing.

"Hi," he said looking directly up at her.

Suzy knew he could see right up her extremely short skirt; in fact she positioned herself above him deliberately so that he could.

"Hi yourself," she answered, acting aloof as though she really wasn't interested in him at all. But in fact, Suzy was quite interested. This was one fine specimen she thought as she watched the muscles in his arms ripple as he lifted a bundle of reinforcement bars up onto his shoulder.

"Heading back to class?" he asked as he threw the bundle down several feet away.

"Maybe," she answered coyly, "What are you doing?"

"Getting ready to lay a foundation," he answered.

Suzy watched him as he gathered up another bundle and moved it. She squatted down at the edge of the landing still holding the railing above her. Her skirt rode up her thighs even further as she opened her legs a bit more and her halter-top rose with her up stretched arms revealing her midriff and above.

"I'll bet you're real good at laying".... pausing, she finished her sentence..."foundations" she cooed with a smirk on her face.

The young man turned slowly and faced her. He walked over to the landing and lowered his eyes to where they were now level with her open legs. He paused for a moment then raising his eyes to meet hers he answered;

"I'm very good."

Suzy seemed to stare longingly into the young mans eyes and then suddenly stood up and spoke.

"Maybe one night when I go into town, we could get together and you could tell me all about laying foundations."

"I'm sure I could explain it to you," he said with a smile.

"I'd have to be back in my dorm by midnight," she added.

"That would be plenty of time," he answered. Clearly he understood her intentions.

"Next week okay?" Suzy asked.

"Sounds good," he answered.

Suzy turned and walked slowly down the steps of the main building. She knew his eyes were glued to her swaying hips squeezed into the material of her ever so tight skirt. There was only a month and a half left before graduation and she wasn't going to waste any of it.

Chapter Two

As she lay there emerging from a deep sleep, she couldn't be sure of what it was she was hearing. Then, Ms. Elsa Duncan realized that there was pounding at her door.

She bolted from the bed and quickly slipping her robe on as she ran she made her way toward her bedroom door.

This was the only part of her job as the girls dorm mother here at Glenridge she didn't particularly relish. She loved all the girls mind you, sometimes as if they were her own, but having to get up at all hours of the night often times proved to be a bit much. Everything from stubbed toes to broken hearts, lost room keys to bad dreams, she had comforted them all. As she approached her door however, something in the frantic tone of the girls voices outside her room told her that this was going to be something more than a stubbed toe. She glanced over at the wall clock. It read 1:30.

She opened the door as three girls virtually tumbled into the room. They were all talking at once and she could sense real fear in their voices. She gathered the girls together and gestured for them to sit down on the couch near the entry way of the room.

"Okay now, one at a time," Elsa asked. "What did you see and where?"

"At the end of the hall," one of the girls blurted out excitedly.

"He was just waiting for us," another of the girls cried out.

"Whoa, whoa now, hold on here," Elsa asked as she

tried to calm the girls down.

"Just exactly what do you think you saw?"

As she caught her breath, one of the girls began;

"At the end of the hall, right by the bathroom, there was this guy just standing there."

She looked around Elsa's apartment as if to make sure the stranger wasn't there with them now.

"Okay, come on now. Let's go take a look shall we?"

Elsa offered, and she and the girls got up and proceeded out into the hallway. The girls fell back behind Elsa as the group made it's way down the hallway. As they turned the corner towards the bathrooms and showers, Elsa turned and asked the girls,

"Do you know what he looked like? Did any of you recognize him? Was he young or older?"

"We really didn't get to see his face," one of the girls answered.

"Yeah, he turned the corner and waited for us. All we saw was his shadow," another of the girls added.

"He was standing right there at the corner," one of the girls went on pointing her finger ahead of them. "Like he was just waiting for us to come by."

Elsa turned and continued walking towards the end of the hall. The girls stayed put and let Elsa go ahead. As she reached the end of the hall, Elsa hesitantly looked around the corner. There was nothing there. The emergency exit was closed tight. She checked, and it was locked from the inside. No one could have come in or out this way without setting off the alarm. There was however a fairly strong pungent odor that made Elsa draw up her finger to block her nostrils a little.

"Is anyone putting their trash out here in the hallway girls?" Elsa asked as she turned back towards the girls.

The girls were huddled together halfway back down the hallway.

"No ma'am, nobody up here has been doing that" one of the girls answered.

"Well, your boogie man or whatever it was is gone now

so you girls get back to your rooms and get some sleep. What were you all doing out here in the first place?" Elsa asked.

"We were just up talking and decided we had to go to the bathroom, so we all went together," came the reply from down the hall.

As Elsa passed them in the hallway and headed back to her apartment, she added, "Let's not have any more nonsense tonight okay girls? Goodnight."

"Thank you Ms. Duncan," they all chimed in.

As Elsa reached her room and was about to open her door, a blood-curdling scream cut through the silence of the night. She froze in place as she felt the hair on the back of her neck go up. Elsa had never heard a scream so frightening. As she ran back towards the direction she believed the scream came from, other girls were now streaming out of their rooms.

"What's the matter!" one girl called out.

"What's going on?" another cried.

"Just stay calm and stay by your rooms," Elsa ordered as she ran past them.

As she rounded the corner once again leading to the bathrooms and showers, there on the floor lay one of the three original girls who had come to Elsa earlier.

"Oh my God!" Elsa cried out as she ran towards the girl lying curled up on the hallway floor.

The girl was unconscious when she knelt down beside her. Other girls were now gathering around the stricken figure on the floor. Elsa picked up her wrist and checked her pulse. It was erratic, but strong.

"Someone run and get the first aid kit out of the shower room," Elsa called out to the gathered crowd.

Someone reached through the crowd and handed Elsa the first aid kit. She popped it open and pulled out some smelling salts. After breaking it open, she passed it back and forth under the girls nose. Momentarily the girl seemed to move and then shudder under the potent aroma of the salts. When she opened her eyes, she drew back as if frightened of something over everyone's shoulders. The girls in the crowd looked all around them to see what it was she was frightened of but there was nothing there.

"What happened sweetheart, tell me," Elsa pleaded, but the girl didn't speak.

Instead she just lay there staring up at the ceiling, her eyes nearly bulging out of their sockets, her entire body shaking uncontrollably.

"She's going into shock," Elsa muttered. Turning towards the crowd of girls she ordered, "Someone call 9-1-1, right now!"

After the paramedics had administered to the girl and were rolling her out to the ambulance on a gurney, Elsa asked the girls still gathered in the hallways if anyone knew if maybe the stricken girl was diabetic. No one seemed to have ever seen any indications that she might have been.

"Besides," one girl asked, "Why would she have screamed out so?"

No one knew or could even guess and so, Elsa hurried the rest of the girls back to their rooms and then walked back towards her own apartment room.

As she reached the end of that hall, she turned and looked back towards the other end where the girls had said they had seen someone…or something.

Elsa dressed and prepaired to drive to the hospital to be with the girl. She had called Mr. Thompson's number and left a message as to what had taken place.

If there were boys sneaking around the girl's dorms trying to scare them, she knew Mr. Thompson would put an end to it right away.

In the morning they would call the girls parents and inform them of what had happened as well.

Suzy Jennings got back to her room with her roommate and they immediately crawled back into their respective beds and fell asleep immediately. All this excitement had tired them out. Something however woke Suzy and as she lay there staring at the ceiling for what now seemed an eternity, she thought *did I really hear that? Or was I dreaming?*

- 12 -

She looked over at the clock on her nightstand. 3:53. She could hear her roommate breathing as she slept across the room.

Why didn't Carol hear that too? She wondered.

There it was again. It began as a low crying type sound, almost like a cat in pain but eerier. Suzy jumped up out of her bed and stood motionless in the middle of the room.

"Do you hear that!" she cried out reaching over and shaking her roommate.

Rubbing her eyes and slowly rolling over onto her side, Carol looked up at Suzy with a frustrated look on her face and asked, "Suzy, it's the middle of the night. What do you want?"

"Shhh...listen," Suzy whispered as she turned around in the room as if to see where the sound might be coming from.

Again it came, only this time it was louder sounding more like the painful cry of a human.

"It's just coyote's out in the woods," Carol said and turned to go back to sleep.

"That's not coyote's." Suzy answered as she walked over to their second story window facing the forest beyond and peered cautiously out into the blackness. She could tell by the trees that no wind was blowing. Suddenly it began again, only this time it grew from a distant crying to an ungodly howling that seemed to be moving towards them. The howling grew louder and louder as it seemed to race closer and closer to the dormitory. Suzy stood clutching the drapes at the window when suddenly the door to her room began to shake violently as though the hallway were a tunnel through which a hurricane force wind was passing through. With it swept a repulsive odor that permeated the room causing her nostrils to flare. Suzy felt faint as she held tightly to the curtains. Suddenly, everything went silent, completely silent. No sounds, save her roommates steady breathing as she slept.

Suzy looked over at Carol with disbelief that she hadn't seemed to hear a thing.

"I must be dreaming," she whispered as she fell onto her bed. "This is unbelievable, I must be dreaming."

"She's still sedated, hasn't really spoken to anyone," Elsa reported as she entered Jack Thompson's office. "I was over there again this morning on my way in. It's really odd; she's completely withdrawn, almost like a coma. Her doctor seems pretty concerned."

"What do you think happened Elsa?" Thompson asked as he stood behind his desk.

Elsa moved across the room and stared out the window. She sighed and then said, "I just don't know. I hadn't left those girls for more than a few minutes."

"Have her parents been notified?" Thompson asked his secretary.

"Yes, last night," Brenda answered. "The father is flying back from a meeting out of town and her mother was at the hospital all night.

"What could she have seen?" Elsa asked herself out loud as she stared out the window.

"Well Elsa," Thompson began, "There's no need making yourself crazy over this. It wasn't your fault. For all we know it could have been one of the boys wearing a Halloween mask or something. Why don't you go back over to the hospital this afternoon and see how she's doing."

Thompson sat down at his desk and began reviewing some papers he had there. Elsa took his actions to signal that there was nothing further to discuss at this time so she turned and walked out of the office.

It was after 2 a.m. Friday night when Suzy locked the door to her room behind her. Carol, being a local girl, always went home for the weekend, thereby allowing Suzy to host whomever she wanted without worry of interruption.

"It sure took you long enough to get here," she scolded as she walked up behind Tim. Tim was her latest conquest. A jock she had been teasing for weeks who was eager to be with her given her reputation around campus.

"They made me do clean-ups after work tonight," He answered. "Where's your roommate?"

"She goes home on the weekends. Why, were you hoping for a threesome?" Suzy laughed as she led Tim over to her bed. She immediately began unbuttoning his shirt.

"Are we in a hurry?" Tim asked as he fell back on to the bed.

"I am," Suzy purred as she reached down and unbuckled Tim's belt.

For the better part of the next two hours Suzy enjoyed what had become a pastime of hers here at Glenridge.

Whoever's idea it was to turn the academy in to a co-ed institution years ago should be awarded she thought, *It made the boys so much more accessible.*

"I'm gonna go rinse off," Suzy whispered as she slipped off the young mans sweating body. Tim watched her glide across the room. He had to admit, this was one night he wasn't going to forget soon. Everything he had heard about Suzy from the other guys was true. She was one wild girl.

Suzy put on her robe and opened the door to her room. The dorm floor was quiet. The other girls were either gone for the weekend or were asleep. Suzy peeked out the door and then back at Tim.

"I'll be right back," she whispered.

The door shut and she disappeared down the hall towards the showers. Tim figured this would be a good time to slip out himself. He'd had enough for one night.

Suzy reached inside the shower room for the light switch. When the lights went on she thought she noticed something move. She stood there for a moment thinking that maybe there was another girl in one of the other stalls taking a shower in the dark. But why no lights she thought. Then she smiled. Maybe she wasn't alone?

"Hey, is anybody else in here?" she called out.

There was no answer so she walked over by the lockers to see if maybe someone was hiding there so as not to be caught off guard. She waited for a moment. When she was satisfied that she probably didn't see anything at all, she walked into the showers.

The hot water felt good on her skin. She closed her eyes and imagined what she and Tim had just been doing. It made her tingle a bit as she could still feel his hands on her. She looked around as though to be sure no one was watching as she continued lathering her body. As she did, the lights suddenly flickered off and on and then off again. Suzy looked around and then up at the darkened light.

"Oh Shit!, just what I need," she muttered.

She wasn't looking forward to a power failure right in the middle of her shower. She turned and reached for her shampoo on the ledge of the shower stall. As she did she seemed to see an unmistakable shadow on the wall of the next shower over.

At first she felt a little frightened as she called out "Who's there?"

Then her fear melted away and a wry smile came across her face as she called out quietly, "Tim? Is that you? Come on in, the waters fine."

She waited for a moment for him to respond. When he didn't, she smiled and figured he probably wanted to slip in beside her after turning off the lights and surprise her.

"Come on over Tim, you and I can make this water even hotter eh?" she cooed.

She looked up as the shadowy figure moved towards the front of the adjacent shower stall. Suzy felt a little shiver of excitement come over her, as she thought about the two of them in the shower together.

Chapter Three

This Saturday morning came way to early for Suzanne. After the movies the night before, she and a couple of her girlfriends had decided to go by the twenty-four hour café for fries and shakes, She didn't get into bed till around 1:30 in the morning which probably wasn't too smart since now she had to get up and get ready for work. Opening the donut shop on the weekends was a nice promotion, but having to be there by 6 a.m. on a Saturday wasn't all that much fun. Still, she couldn't complain, the two gals that actually made the donuts had to be there by 4:30. She glanced over at her clock. 5:14, just enough time to shower, get dressed and drive up to the shop on the highway in town. Still, she hated having to get up this early. As she rounded the corner in the hallway, she noticed the lights were on in the showers. Ms. Duncan, their dorm mother was always getting on the girls for leaving the lights on in the showers. She had even threatened to put in a timer. Suzanne could see where at least last night might have been a good time to have one. As Suzanne turned and walked into the shower room, she stopped suddenly in her tracks as she looked into the stall areas. *Oh great, we've been vandalized* she thought.

It appeared that someone had smeared red paint all over the tile in one of the shower stalls. It was clear up to the ceiling and outside on the tile floor. Right away Suzanne figured it was probably the senior boys as they were always coming up with some sort of prank on the girls.

She stood there for a few moments staring at the mess.

It looked a little strange she thought as she approached the stall. It really didn't look like paint. As she got closer an eerie feeling came over her. She was hesitant to go further but she did anyway. Suzanne walked around the corner. She felt a wave of nausea sweep over her entire body. She tried to scream but it wouldn't come. She froze and started shaking. Then it came; it rose from the deepest part of her body. Suzanne screamed and screamed and screamed.

***

Sheriff James Fremont stood motionless in the shower. All of his years in Homicide back in Los Angeles hadn't prepared him for what he was seeing this morning. It was everywhere, as though an abstract artist had simply spewed buckets of crimson paint across the walls, ceiling and floor. Except it wasn't paint, it was blood. Instead it was a work of horror. The young girls body had been impaled upon the showerhead, her breasts had been sheared off her body and strewn across the shower floor like two pieces of meat. Her legs had been so brutally stretched apart in a grotesque fashion and gaping hole had been torn open between them. She had been literally gutted and her insides were lying in a pile beneath her.

James could hear the sound of at least two of his deputies throwing up in the next stall from what they had seen.

"This is sick, Jimmy, real sick," a voice spoke from behind him.

Jim turned around to see Dr. Mark Turner the Medical Examiner standing there with his hand cupping his chin.

"Your boys thought I should get a look at this before they took it down,"

"What do you think of this?" Jim asked.

"I don't know Jimmy, but somebody sure as hell really didn't like this girl," Turner answered as he opened his bag.

Fremont turned and addressed his deputies who were still trying to regain their composure in the locker room, "I don't want any details of this out to the press you understand?"

"Okay boss," two voices answered in unison from outside the showers.

"Where's the girl that found her?" Jim asked again addressing the deputies that were outside of the shower area.

"They took her over to Holy Cross. She went into shock pretty bad," a deputy answered.

Jim turned and walked out into the hallway where there were several more deputies standing.

"Did anybody else see or hear anything?" he asked.

"Nobody heard a thing sir," one of the men answered.

"Somebody saw her last night out with one of the boys that go here. We haven't found out who he is yet, though," another deputy added.

Jim proceeded down the hall to the dead girl's room.

When he entered it there were several officers already combing through the room.

"Find anything Phil?" Jim asked.

Phil Barlow was one of the oldest men on Jim's staff. Twenty-five years here in Glenridge and one of the best cops Jim had ever seen. There were few as good even back in L.A..

"Well ya know Jim, from the looks of things in here I'd say the last thing she did in this room was have sex."

Jim nodded, turned and walked out of the room. He spoke with one of his deputies that had just returned from the showers.

"You okay?" he asked.

"Yeah, but that was pretty bad in there," he answered.

"Okay, well I want this boyfriend found and brought in right away," Jim ordered.

"We'll find him," the deputy replied.

The two men walked down the hall and out into the bright early morning sun. Outside the building crowds of students woken by the sirens and commotion had now gathered. A news crew was just arriving and one of the reporters ran up to Jim. Shoving a microphone towards Jim he asked, "Can you tell us exactly what happened in there Chief, some of your people are saying it was pretty horrible in there."

"No comment at this time," he answered as he pushed his way through the crowd to his car.

By now several of the construction crew working on the restoration had arrived for work and seeing the commotion, had walked over to the dorms.

Jim turned to them and asked "How long have you guys been working on the campus?"

"Just about a week or so. Why?" one of the men answered.

"Seen anybody around that looks out of the ordinary" Jim asked.

"No, just students and faculty," another man answered.

As Jim and the deputy reached the car, the deputy turned to Jim and said, "Boss, did you see that girls hair? Those white streaks?"

Jim nodded. He figured she must have seen something horribly frightening to do that.

It was now almost 9 a.m. when Jim finally sat down at his desk.

"Well, what have we got so far?" Jim asked as two of his deputies walked into his office.

"So far we still haven't found the boy, but several of the girls at the dorm say it was just a matter of time before she'd bring the wrong guy home," one of the men answered.

The other officer added "Apparently our Ms. Jennings liked picking up guys from all over the area, not just other students, and bringing them back to her dorm room. It was a pretty regular occurrence."

Jim sifted through some of his notes until he found the one he was looking for.

"So what about this kid someone saw her with last night, this Tim Patricks?" Jim asked as he threw the notes down on the desk.

One of the deputies looked at his notes and answered, "He's clean. No record, gets good grades, plays baseball for the school and everybody seems to like him, even his teachers."

"So where is he?" Jim asked.

"According to his roommate, he didn't sleep there last night and his travel bag is gone. We've got everybody looking for him, even State," came the answer.

Jim got up and walked over to his window. The view of the mountains suddenly didn't seem so pretty this morning. Someone had dirtied up the landscape with this heinous crime.

Still staring out the window, Jim instructed his men, "I want you to call State and get a list of any sex offenders in the area. Also, anyone with an M.O. like this that might have been recently released from custody from anywhere and traveling in this direction. I also want backgrounds on any boyfriends or people this girl may have been with while she was going to this school."

"Right Chief," the men said as they left Jim's office leaving him staring out the window.

"You wanted to see me boss?" a voice came from over Jim's shoulder.

Jim turned and saw Phil Barlow standing in the doorway. As many years as Phil had been here Jim learned that Phil was an invaluable source of information about the area and it's inhabitants.

"Come on in and sit down Phil," Jim said as he gestured to the chair across from his desk.

Being the oldest member of Jim's staff and still carrying a bullet fragment in his hip from an incident many years ago, Phil moved a little slower than most, but as Jim had learned early on, there was no one more thorough in an investigation.

"What do you know about that janitor out there at the academy?" Jim asked.

"Who, Conrad? He's the last person I'd worry about Jim. He's been out at the school for about as long as I can remember. Granted, he's a little odd but I'd trust him with my mother," Phil answered.

"There were a couple of complaints last year about somebody hanging out around the girls dorm. His name came up as I recall," Jim said.

"Yeah, I remember but I still say he's not your man," Phil replied.

Jim felt comfortable with Phil's conviction. The janitor really didn't seem to make sense, but Jim had to consider every possibility.

"So have you got any theories about this?" Jim queried.

Phil leaned back in the chair and answered, "I don't know Jim, this is without a doubt one of the worst killings I've ever seen or even heard of in all my years in law enforcement. Whoever did this is real sick, real perverted and real mad. I'll tell you one thing though; it's not even four hours since this broke and it sure has brought everybody out of the woodwork."

"What do you mean?" Jim asked curiously.

"Well, besides all the armchair quarterbacks over at Brady's barber shop, there's an old fortune teller lady that lives way out off Mill Road in the woods out there. Haven't seen her in town in over ten years. She must be in her late sixties at least, by now. Most people around here figure she's a little touched, you know what I mean, but there she was, sitting out in front of Millers store this morning."

"Think she came into town to solve our murder?" Jim asked jokingly.

"Don't laugh, a lot of people used to visit her little cabin out there in the woods and get their fortunes told. She used to have a little sign on the highway for years. A lot of people thought she was pretty accurate until she started foreseeing some weird stuff and kind of fell out of grace you might say. People stopped going out there. The sign disappeared and she just stopped coming into town."

"How does she get food and stuff out there?" Jim asked.

"Somebody from around here gets it for her we think. Nobody knows who for sure though," Phil answered as he shifted in the chair, the old wound making it difficult for him to sit in one position for too long.

Jim looked up as one of his deputies poked his head into the doorway.

"What do you want us to tell these guys from the press boss?" he asked.

"Tell them we've got some strong leads and we're working on them," he answered.

Turning his attention back to Phil he added, "Maybe we should call in the psychic and see who she thinks did this."

***

Jim wasn't sure if he was dreaming or if in fact the phone was ringing. He slowly turned his head towards the nightstand and looked at the time. 5:17 a.m.. He reached over and fumbled with the receiver for a moment until finally raising it to his ear.

"Sorry to wake you so early Sheriff," the voice on the other end said. "But we've got another dead girl out here at the academy."

Jim blinked his eyes open wider and answered, "I'll be right there."

"What is it?" Jim's wife asked groggily as she reached up and turned the bedside lamp on.

"I've got to go honey. Go back to sleep," he answered her and reached over to turn the light off.

The brutality of the girl's death yesterday morning seemed to pale in comparison to the scene before Jim now. The pale light of the oncoming sunrise revealed more than any of them were ready for so soon.

The girl's head was twisted grotesquely on her

shoulders as if someone had actually tried to rip it off. She hung from the raised arm of the backhoe, her skull skewered by the tooth of the blade on the shovel. The front of her was soaked in blood. Laying on the ground beneath her was a bloodied 3-inch round stake, one end broken off leaving only a jagged edge. It was covered in the dark remains of the girls life giving fluid.

"Hey there's more blood up here," one of the deputies called out from the landing of the wrought iron stairway leading up to the second story of the girl's dorm.

Jim walked up the stairs to where the deputy stood. He inspected the landing and the locked door. He now looked down at the horrific sight below as his men and the emergency personnel strained to dislodge the girl's head from the tooth of the back hoe and lower her to the ground. He walked back down the staircase and over to where the girl's mutilated body had been placed on an open body bag. Dr. Turner was now kneeling over the body as he approached.

"Well Mark, I guess we're keeping you pretty busy," Jim said.

Mark Turner looked up at Jim and then back down at the dead girl's body without saying a word. He got up and motioned to the EMS personnel to go ahead and close her up and remove her to his office.

"I'll get you what I can before sun up Jim," Mark said as he turned and walked to his car.

Jim looked up at the raised arm of the backhoe and knew he wouldn't be through here for quite awhile.

He walked over to one of the deputies and looking out over the crowd that was gathering asked, "Who found this one?"

"Security. When he drove by around 4:00," came the answer.

"Anybody see or hear anything?" Jim continued.

"A girl in the dorm thought she saw something around 1:30 when she was going to the bathrooms," the deputy added.

"I want to talk to her. Where is she?" Jim asked.

"In her room up in the dorm," the deputy answered leading the way as Jim followed him.

The girl was sitting on the edge of her bed talking with one of the female deputies when they walked in. The deputy got up as Jim pulled the girl's desk chair up in front of the girl and sat down.

"What's your name Miss?" Jim asked gently.

"Angela," she answered

"I understand you saw someone in the building tonight?" Jim queried.

"Well, not exactly," she began. "I was going to the bathroom and I thought I saw someone down at the end of the hall, but actually all I really saw was his shadow. There must have been someone there, but I wasn't sure. I really didn't see them. I figured it was nothing since no one can get in or out that way without anyone knowing."

The female deputy jumped in at this point adding "One of the other girls I spoke with here on this floor said that she and her girlfriends thought they saw someone down at the end of the hallway the other night also. Scared one of them so bad, paramedics had to take her to the hospital to try and calm her down. She's still there, apparently completely withdrawn. Won't speak to anyone. She's like in a comatose state."

"Where are these other girls?" Jim asked as he got up from the chair.

"Back in their rooms I suppose," the deputy answered.

"I want to see them in my office this morning. You come back here and pick them up and drive them over okay?" Jim said.

"I will sir," the deputy answered.

"Okay Angela, I appreciate your staying here and answering our questions," Jim said as he shook the young girl's hand. "Maybe you can get some sleep now."

"Are you kidding?" she answered in a voice bordering on hysteria, "Nobody getting much sleep around here with this maniac out there. When are you gonna catch him?"

"I'm not sure," Jim muttered as he turned to leave the girls room.

"I don't care what they said about her. She didn't deserve to die like that," Angela said now sobbing.

Jim stopped suddenly and turned back and addressed the girl on the bed.

"What exactly do you mean by that? What did you say?"

Angela looked up and wiping her tears answered, "Oh, a lot of us thought she was.... well...pretty loose you might say. You know, fooled around a lot. But she shouldn't have had to die that way. I mean what kind of animal does that to a girl?"

Jim stood and listened and then turned and walked out of the room. As he left he turned to his deputies gathered there and ordered, "I want this campus searched completely, every nook and cranny. Anything that looks suspicious, I want to know about it immediately."

"Yes sir," came the reply almost in unison as they all dispersed.

Jim walked down the flight of stairs and back outside into the now dawning sunlight. He glanced over at where the body of the girl was found at the side of the building. He knew that time was critical here in catching whoever was committing these horrible crimes. Not only could the person or persons strike again, but also the effect on the campus as well as the town was growing.

He walked over to his car and drove over to Turner's office.

The sun was now peeking over the hillside as he pulled up. After knocking on the front door for several minutes, a weary eyed man opened it.

"Come on in Chief, I've got some coffee on if you want," Turner said as he led the way back to his examining room.

As the two men entered the brightly lit room, Jim noticed the covered remains of the girl from yesterday's killing.

On a table in the middle of the room lay the latest victim. He walked up to the table and saw what couldn't be seen out at the crime scene. Her breasts had been bludgeoned into a mass of bruised and battered flesh.

"That's not even the beginning," Turner said as he walked around the table. "It seems our boy smashed her chest repeatedly over and over with that baseball bat before it apparently broke. Then he rammed the broken end up inside her a couple hundred times as hard as he could until there was nothing left inside her. Her insides just poured out onto the ground. Then he somehow plunged her head onto that backhoe that was sitting there. I'm telling you Jimmy, you've got a real sick individual on your hands here."

"Hate? Revenge? Simply mental?" Jim asked out loud, "What causes someone to be so violent?"

Jim stood there for a few moments looking down at the remains of a face that only yesterday was probably a happy girl away at college. He remembered seeing hookers slashed and beat up back in L.A. by their "Johns" or "Pimps" for whatever reason. The sight always made him sick in the beginning, but as the consistency continued, he became more callused to it until finally it was no different that looking at cut up meat on the butchers counter. But now here in this small town, the sight once again made him feel sick and uncertain. What type of animal was loose out there? Why was he picking on these girls at this place? Was it random or was the similarity in each girl's sexual behavior a key.

He turned to Mark and said, "Let me know if you find anything else."

Once outside he took several deep breaths of the crisp morning air. He slid onto the seat of the cruiser and radioed the office that he was going home and grab a quick shower and would be in shortly.

"Copy that Chief," came the dispatchers reply.

As he toweled his hair dry, the two crimes played themselves over and over in his mind. He clearly needed some help with this one. He walked into the bedroom and picked up the phone and dialed long distance.

"Dr. Lansbury's office," the voice on the other end answered.

"Is Dr. Lansbury in?" he asked as he tightened the towel around his waist.

"I'm sorry sir, but Ms. Lansbury won't be in until ten this morning. May I take a message?" the voice asked.

"Yes, please ask her to call James Fremont as soon as she gets in would you? She has my number."

Jim hung up the phone. He knew if anyone could help profile this killer, Judith Lansbury could. She worked closely with the L.A.P.D. and had worked with Jim on several cases back there over the years.

He dressed quickly and drove over to his office. In his six years since taking the job here, Jim had never seen the office so busy. All the lines were ringing, news crews from as far away as Sacramento were hanging out in an office provided to them and there were people all over the waiting room. As he walked into his office, three deputies followed.

"Who are all those people out there?" he asked as he hung his jacket on the wooden rack behind his desk.

"Most of them are worried parents, some reporters and the rest are just folks from town wanting to know what's going on," one of the deputies answered.

Another deputy sat down on the wooden bench against the wall and opened up a file folder.

"Here's what I've got so far on known sex offenders in the area," he began. "Only two men are currently listed as living within a seventy-five mile radius of here. One of them is currently in New York visiting an aunt and the other one is at home. He lives on a small ranch about six miles out of town. I've got Simpson going out there for him."

A second deputy standing now in front of Jim's desk began, "I went ahead and checked to see if we had any new

- 28 -

arrivals in town lately like you asked and I found three. One is a Ms. Betty Wiltern. She's the new third grade teacher over at the elementary school. The other is Fred Shipley's brother. He's visiting from Nebraska for a week."

"Who's the third one?" Jim asked.

"His name is Bob Mifflin. I don't have anything on him yet, but I've got Roger keeping an eye on him. So far he doesn't seem to have done anything out of the ordinary except ask a lot of folks a lot of questions."

"Questions? What about?" Jim asked.

"He seems to be looking for someone," the deputy answered.

Jim continued, "What do we have on that boy that was with the Jennings girl?"

"We haven't found him yet," the third deputy answered. "But we have spoken with his parents in Tucson and they haven't heard from him."

"I think he's our boy chief," one of the deputies interjected, "Why else would he suddenly disappear?"

"Well, I don't know, but until we have something concrete let's all keep our eyes and ears open and maybe I'll have a little chat with that new guy who's asking all the questions" Jim said.

"You want we should bring him in boss?" one of the deputies asked.

"No, let's not spook him just yet. If you see him around town call me and I'll approach him and strike up a conversation with him," Jim answered.

Another deputy stuck his head in the doorway and said

"Chief? I've got a Ms. Lansbury on line two for you. Says she's from L.A.?"

Chapter Four

The old woman sat motionless in the dark corner as the flames from the stone fireplace cast eerie shadows around the room of the old cabin. One of the shadows moved slowly across the room to the small kitchenette adjacent to the front room.

"I've put all the food away in the same places," a voice spoke softly. "You shouldn't have any trouble finding anything."

"You seem troubled my dear. Come sit by the fire here before you leave," the old woman's crackling voice said as she patted the cushion next to her.

Obediently the shadow of a woman moved across the room and sat down next to the old lady.

"You're troubled more than usual tonight," the old woman said as she placed her withered hand upon the other woman's arm and continued staring into the fire.

The woman looked down at the wrinkled hand upon her arm. For so many years this old gypsy could sense whatever she was feeling. It was uncanny how she knew when she was troubled.

"You remember years ago when I told you your nightmares would end?" the old woman said, never taking her eyes off the crackling fire before her.

"But I thought it would be me," the woman whispered.

"It's not always as you think," the old woman replied.

They both sat in silence for a long time. Finally, the woman got up and quietly left the cabin, leaving the old gypsy still staring at the fire. As she left, she looked back at the cabin. An overwhelming feeling of fear swept over her as he got into her car.

This was no ordinary Sunday morning at Glenridge Academy. The fear that everyone there felt was growing each passing day that the killer was still loose. Parents were arriving hourly to take their children home despite the efforts of the chancellor and his staff to try and assure them that every effort was being taken to ensure the student's safety.

Word of the grizzly attacks were adding to the fear even though they were being controlled as best they could by the sheriff's office.

As parents vented their frustration with the administration over what they felt was the lack of proper security measures, students gathered in clusters speculating on who might be responsible. Some thought it might be one of the male students there at the academy while others thought it was a stranger lurking in the woods, while at least one other student was certain it was Jason Voorhees from the Friday the 13th movie.

Not all the students were preoccupied with the murders though.

"I don't know Liz, there's cops and security everywhere now and I heard they're going to enforce an early curfew. Maybe we'd better cool it for awhile," Paul argued.

Liz turned and walked a few steps away and then turned and looked back at Paul.

"Are you telling me you don't want to?" she asked coyly. "Heck, this is a great opportunity," she continued. "My roommates leaving in an hour. She called her parents this morning and they told her to get home right away. We can have the whole room all to ourselves all night."

"I just don't think it's all that safe," Paul said as he sat down on the steps of the old administration building.

"Fine, you want to do it in your room?" Liz asked impatiently.

Paul nodded dejectedly. They both knew they couldn't go up to his room. When Liz first started her affair with Paul they had tried his room but with his roommate always there and all the traffic his room saw every night, it proved impossible.

"Then let's go somewhere else," Liz said.

"Where?" Paul asked.

Liz sat down next to Paul on the steps and looked upward. The sunlight glared off the window at the top of the old building.

"How about up there?" she offered.

Paul looked up. Then standing up in front of Liz he answered.

"Nobody's allowed in that building after hours much less getting up there. Too risky."

"A little risk makes it all that more exciting," she answered. "Besides, if anything does happen, we can watch it all from up there."

"How are we gonna get in there. They keep that building locked up at night," Paul asked as he walked up the steps towards the entrance.

Liz got up and ran up the stairs after him.

"You leave that part up to me. Just be here at midnight tonight," Liz giggled as she turned and went back to the girls' dorm.

Jim usually went home for lunch, but when his deputy radioed that the Mifflin boy just went into Lucy's coffee shop and he was right around the corner, he figured it might be a good time to have a talk with him. He pulled the cruiser up in front of the café and went inside.

"Could you pass me that menu?" Jim asked as he sat down at the counter. The young man seated next to him

- 32 -

handed the menu to Jim and smiled.

"I haven't seen you around here before," Jim said, "Are you just passing through?"

"No sir. I have a few days off from work and I thought I'd come up here and try to get some information," the young man answered.

"Information? What kind of information?" Jim asked.

"An Uncle of mine disappeared from up here back in 1965. I wanted to see if I could find out anything about it," he answered, adding, "Maybe you could help me?"

"I've only been here about six years, but I have a few officers that have been here a pretty long time. Maybe one of them can assist you," Jim offered. "What was his name?"

"John Mifflin. He went to school up here. An all boys academy?" the young man answered.

Mifflin went on to tell the story of how just before the end of his freshman year in High School, his uncle just disappeared from sight. He had left all his belongings at the school and just vanished. Apparently the search went on for months but nothing ever came of it. He went on to explain how his own father had been consumed by the loss of his brother so mysteriously so many years before and until his sudden death from a heart attack last year, he had spent all his time trying to find out what happened.

"I just thought I would come up here and see if there was anything my dad might have missed," Mifflin said.

"You're probably talking about Roundhill," Jim said, "It was an all boys school a couple of miles down the road from Glenridge. They folded the boys academy into one co-ed academy at Glenridge in the mid-seventies. Have you been out to there yet?" Jim asked.

"Not yet," the young man answered almost hesitating.

Jim already knew the boy had been out there since one of his deputies had already reported seeing him there the day before. Why was this young man now lying to him he wondered.

"Why don't you come on over to my office and we can

look up some old files and see if we can find anything," Jim offered.

"Thanks," Mifflin said "I'll try to get over there this afternoon," he added.

Jim was disappointed that he couldn't get the young man to come right away but he wanted to put together a little more information on him before he could consider him a prime suspect. With that, Jim got up and walked out of the cafe into the bright afternoon sun. He hadn't taken two steps when one of his deputies pulled up in front.

Through the open passenger window he shouted out to Jim, "They need you back at the office Chief, right away."

Jim waved and acknowledged the request, then stepped up to his own cruiser and got in. He was just pulling out of the diagonal parking space when he noticed Mifflin coming out of the café. He stepped out into the sunlight and without looking over at Jim, hurriedly walked away down the street. Jim watched as he disappeared around the corner wondering if he was watching his murderer walk. His story had seemed plausible and it was the only reason Jim let him alone at this time.

"Hang on to your Smokey boss," a deputy said as Jim entered the station. "Your lunch buddy may in fact be our boy."

Jim's heart sank as he thought that he might have just let the suspect walk away from him. He entered his office as the excited deputy followed.

"Shut the door," Jim said in case there might be some over zealous ears from the press out there.
"It seems," the deputy continued, " Our visitor had a little scrape with the law a few times. Once, when he was nineteen, he was arrested for stalking a supposed girlfriend. Stockton P.D. tells us that he apparently got "into it" with a girl there and punched her. She was a senior in high school at the time. Then again in '87, he was picked up in Denver along with several others in connection with the murder of a hooker. The witnesses couldn't I.D. him though so he walked. Here's

where it gets real interesting though. The hooker in Denver was the mother of the girl in Stockton.

"What was the disposition in Stockton?" Jim asked.

"The girl and her then step-mother didn't pursue any charges so he walked on that one too," the deputy answered.

"Okay, but it still doesn't explain why he would come here and go bat shit all over the campus," Jim argued folding his hands under his chin and stretching back in his chair.

Jim reached forward and retrieved notes from on top of his desk.

"Listen to this," he began, "I spent a long time on the phone this morning with an old associate of mine from my L.A.P.D. days. She's a criminal psychologist and she's also one of the best at putting together criminal profiles. She seems to think we're looking for someone who is extremely angry with women to start with. Especially one's who are overly sexual. She thinks that young women may have abused our suspect either as a child or as an adult. He must have an intense hatred for young women because of their sexuality. Thus, the brutality of the murders. So far our newcomer here seems to only have a penchant for minor assault and being in the wrong place at the wrong time. Unless he snapped, these crimes don't seem to match his past, although a lot of time has gone by and a lot could have happened to him since. But don't forget, we also have another missing boy that was with the first victim," Jim said.

Jim got up from his desk and walked around to the deputy and placing his arm on the deputy's shoulder continued, "We've definitely got a few good leads. Let's keep pursuing them."

"Right chief," the deputy answered. He turned and opened the office door. As he walked through it, he turned and added, "Oh by the way, your wife called while you were out."

"Thanks," Jim said as the deputy closed the door behind him.

Emily, or "M" as Jim had always called her, was cleaning up the broken dish their cat had just knocked off the counter when the front door opened.

"I'm in the kitchen," Jim heard her call out.

He gave her a pat on her behind as he walked past her to the refrigerator.

"Hi stranger," she said as she came up behind him and encircled his waist with her arms.

"I'm sorry honey, but you know the last few days have been crazy here," he apologized.

"I thought we moved away from all this," she said sadly.

Jim turned and took his wife in his arms. Holding her head against his chest, he gazed out the window and said, "Apparently it's come to visit."

Through dinner Jim explained what was going on with the case. It had become his best form of release when he was with the force back in L.A., Emily had always said that she wanted to be a part of his work. So many other cops could never communicate their feelings about the job with their spouses and often times that proved to be the ruination of perfectly good marriages. Jim and M spent the rest of the evening discussing the case; the possible suspects and the color Emily wanted Jim to paint the family room.

It was eight minutes after twelve when Paul arrived at the back of the main administrative building.

"Where were you?" Liz whispered angrily as he came up to her.

"Relax," he whispered back, "I'm only a few minutes late. Did you figure out how we're supposed to get in there?"

"Follow me," she answered.

The two of them quietly crept around the back of the building. Stacks of scaffolding were propped up against what appeared to be an old service entrance. Liz clambered over the pile and grabbed the handle of the large door.

"Come on, give me a hand," she demanded quietly.

"Are you crazy? If any of that stuff falls, somebody's going to hear us," Paul whispered.

"Then just be careful," Liz quietly giggled.

Paul shook his head in disgust, but nevertheless went over to where Liz was already trying to lift several pieces of scaffolding away from the door. The weight of the heavy iron bars made it very hard to budge.

"I've got a crowbar in my truck," Paul offered.

"Nah, come on. We can do it," Liz insisted as she continued trying to pull the door open.

Paul pulled with her until the door was finally able to be opened just enough for them to squeeze in. As they entered, Paul reached down with one hand and pulled a piece of the metal rod between the door and the jam. He felt a little safer knowing that their exit would already be open for them when they returned.

Without saying a word, Liz reached back taking Paul's hand and led him through the service entry and into the dark hallway of the basement.

"Where are we going?" Paul whispered.

"Upstairs," she answered.

They reached the door leading to the stairwell between the floors. It too was a heavy metal door and it squeaked eerily. Once in the stairwell, they hurriedly climbed to the main floor. Liz stopped when they reached the door and held the handle to the door for several moments.

"Why are we going in here?" Paul asked.

"It's the only way to the attic," she answered.

She pulled the door open slowly and they entered the cavernous hallway of the main administration building. Ahead of them rose the huge wooden stairway to the second floor and beyond that, the attic. As they began to slowly and quietly creep across the entry, Paul glanced down the hallway towards the offices. He noticed something moving, a shadow against the wall. Perhaps that of a tree outside a window, but there were no windows in the hallway. As the shadow continued to move in his own direction he became even more concerned.

"Somebody's in here," he whispered tugging on Liz's blouse.

"Where?" she muttered stopping to turn around.

Paul pointed down the hall where the shadow seemed to be getting larger on the wall.

"What is that?" she whispered.

"Maybe it's the janitor?" Paul offered nervously.

"Can't be. Not this late," Liz said.

"Let's hide," Paul whispered.

They both slipped across the hallway and tried several doors until they found one that was open. Once inside the dark room, they tried to feel their way around. It was pitch black and they had no idea where they were.

"We're gonna get nailed. I just know it," Paul muttered.

As their eyes began to acclimate to the darkness, they crouched down behind some chairs. They waited in silence for about five minutes before venturing out from and stealthily walking back towards the door. They stopped and listened for several more moments. Not hearing anything, they figured that whoever was out there had gone.

"Come on, let's get the heck out of here," Paul said as he reached for the door.

Just as his hand touched the knob, they both felt a strong draft sweep through the door carrying with it a disgusting odor that now filled the entire room. It forced them back away from the door.

"Oh God, What died out there!" Liz gasped as she covered her nose and mouth with her hand.

Paul felt a wave of nausea come over him as he felt as though he would vomit.

"What the hell is that?" he half choked on his words.

He attempted to reach for the knob again but was repelled back again by an even stronger onslaught of the vile and disgusting odor from outside the door. Suddenly they began to hear what sounded like a low growling moan from some distance away. The growl turned to a howling scream and grew closer and closer until it sounded as though a tornado of horror was right outside the door. Now the door began shaking and bulging as though it were a living-breathing thing. Liz grabbed Paul and clutched him tightly as absolute fear coursed through both their bodies. Paul tried grabbing the doorknob but each time he reached for it, the screams would intensify as he did. He finally was able to hold on to the doorknob and turn it, but the door wouldn't open. He pulled harder but it still wouldn't budge. By now the sound of the howling and the shaking door was deafening.

"Shit!, we're trapped in here," Paul yelled.

"I'm scared!" Liz yelled back as she stood behind him shaking and sobbing.

Paul released the doorknob and turned back to Liz. He put his arms around her and held her tightly never taking his eyes off the doorknob. Paul looked up at the small window above the door. It was closed and locked but he could make out the shadow of something moving outside the door.

Suddenly the door flew open crashing against the wall behind it. There was nothing there. The howling stopped just as suddenly along with the odor. The two frightened students stood clutching each other shaking. There was not a sound. The eerie silence was now as terrifying as what they had just moments before experienced. Paul stepped forward first, peering outside the door, first one-way, and then the other. There was nothing there and no sign that anything had been.

"I don't know who this asshole is that's doing this, but we're getting the hell out of here," he said angrily as he led Liz back to the door they had entered the hallway from.

They almost fell several times as they raced down the stairwell to the basement. They ran through the basement to the service entrance and up to the door they had come in.

When they got there Paul stopped short. The door he had deliberately left propped open for their retreat was now closed. He didn't want to stop and try to figure out who or why it had been shut so instead he ran headlong into it putting all his weight behind pushing the door open. Fortunately, he was able to get it open just enough for them both to slip through.

As they ran, they heard the stacked up scaffolding slam the door shut behind them. They ran from the building and didn't stop until they reached the dorm parking lot. There it was brightly lit and they figured they were safe. Both out of breath, Liz spoke first.

"Who the hell was that in there," she cried.

"I don't know. Some jerk trying to scare us," Paul answered angrily as he tried to catch his breath as well.

"Well they did a real good job as far as I'm concerned," Liz added.

"Maybe it was the murderer," Paul said in a haunting voice trying to scare Liz.

Liz punched him hard in the arm and said sarcastically "Cute! Real cute. I'm going back to the dorm."

"I'll walk you back" Paul offered as he put his arm around her shoulder. "You know, we can't tell anybody about this or we'll get busted for being in there at night" he added.

"I don't think anybody would believe it anyway," Liz answered as they walked back to the dorms.

Chapter Five

Most of the classes seemed eerily quiet and smaller in size on Monday morning. Many students had left either voluntarily or had been summoned home by their parents. Conversations were less about academics and more about the gruesome murders. Everyone, it seemed had a theory about who it might be, from the weird Biology teacher, to any guy on campus who hadn't gotten laid in a long time. Someone had even started a rumor that it might be Bigfoot coming out from the woods to take revenge for messing with the forests of the world. The mood was much the same in town with everyone second-guessing as to suspicious people. Jim Fremont wasn't second-guessing though. He had two strong leads, which his deputies were following up on as he sat in the town council offices above the fire station.

"Look Jim," the Mayor said, "We've gotta do something soon. Have you seen those news crews out there? Need I remind you, an awful lot of tourists come up here every summer and even more on the weekends? If this gets out on the wire services, we're gonna have every T.V. network within 500 miles up here blasting out news that we have some crazed killer running loose among the pine trees. Wouldn't make people want to be in a big hurry to come up here now would it Jim boy?"

"I can't stop them from being here," Jim answered.

He knew how this mayor was, and dollars and cents seemed to always be his priority. Maybe that was one of the reasons nobody liked him.

"No," the mayor continued. "But maybe you could let it out that that you're gonna make an arrest real soon. Might put their minds at ease a little?"

"And just who exactly would you like me to arrest?" Jim asked.

Whenever city officials brought pressure to bear upon a case that was difficult to solve, it always meant rushing things and that usually led to sloppy work. Jim had seen too much of that back in L.A., and he wasn't going to let that happen here.

"I can probably keep the news people at bay for a little while longer," Jim offered. "But understand this. I'm not real close to any arrest and no one had better imply to anyone that my office is."

With that Jim turned and walked out of the Mayor's office. As he descended the steps and walked out into the morning sunlight, he hoped that it wouldn't be too long before he could change that answer.

Across town, Emily Fremont sat with three of her girlfriends sipping coffee before her next class resumed at the junior college. Taking this course to become a certified nursing assistant was something Emily had always wanted to do. Now that Kevin, their son, was grown with a family of his own, she had plenty of time to pursue her own dream. Once she received her certificate, she could help out down at the hospital. She already knew everyone down there anyway from Jim's work, so she had already made enough inquiries to set things up for herself. In fact it was at the hospital that she met Jill some four years ago. Maria had also become friends with the girls at church and although she was much more quiet and introverted, they had been able to convince her to join them from time to time for lunches and other outings occasionally.

"Fred wants me to stay pretty close to the house this week what with all that's going on over at the academy," Jill said.

"I know. My neighbor's not letting her girls go outside to play," Maria added as she poured herself another cup of tea from the decanter left on the table.

"How far along are they M? Have they got any idea as to who it might be?" Jill asked.

"Jim told me they have a couple of strong leads but nothing definitive," she answered.

"Anybody we would know?" Maria added.

"No, not really. One's a student who seems to have disappeared, and they're watching another guy who arrived in town last week. Apparently though that guy just seems to be looking for his uncle that disappeared up here some years ago and was never found," Emily answered.

"Doesn't Jim have enough going on without having to try and find a missing person?" Jill asked.

"Oh, he'll probably have someone else in the office look into it," Emily said.

"How long ago did this guy's uncle disappear?" Maria asked, her interest clearly piqued, as she set the tea decanter carefully down on the table.

"I think Jim said it was around '65. He went to that all boys school down from Glenridge before they went co-ed," Emily answered.

"I think I remember hearing about that. They never found the guy after months of searching. They even dragged the lake for weeks," Jill said.

Maria sat back in her chair. Her face grew pale and she seemed to be staring off into space. Looking as though she might faint, nevertheless she suddenly got up and bolted towards the ladies room. Emily and Jill watched in amazement as she raced across the coffee shop.

"Is she okay?" Jill asked.

"I don't know. I'll go check on her," Emily answered as she got up and made her way to the ladies room.

"Hey, Maria?" she called out as she entered the ladies room.

Maria was standing at the sink, her hands grasping the counter staring into the mirror. Emily could see that she was crying. She rushed up to her and placing her arm over her shoulder.

"Maria, what's the matter? Don't you feel well?"

"I'm fine, really. I'll be okay," Maria answered as she wiped her tears with the hand towel.

"You don't look fine. In fact you look like you've just seen a ghost. You're white as a sheet. You're not going to faint are you?" Emily asked.

Maria turned and half-heartedly smiled at Emily, then turned and walked out of the restroom.

Emily stood there for a moment wondering what could have caused her friend to suddenly behave that way. When she returned to the table she looked around as she sat back down next to Jill.

"Where's Maria? Didn't she come back?" Emily asked still looking around the restaurant expecting to see their friend returning.

"No. Is she okay?" Jill asked.

"I'm not sure," Emily said with a worried tone in her voice.

"Did we say something wrong?" Jill added.

"I don't think so," Emily answered "I hope she'll be okay."

But Maria wasn't okay. And she probably wasn't going to be okay ever again she thought. Unable to move or even think rationally now she just sat in her car shaking uncontrollably. The images of her husband and her children flashed before her now. She looked out at the large cedar home in front of here and remembered the first day she and her husband, Steve, had moved into it so long ago. Back then it seemed their lives were perfect and that nothing could ever disturb the happiness that filled their days. Now she felt as though a dark and ominous presence stalked her. She wanted to cry, she wanted to scream. She couldn't do either. Instead of going back into the coffee shop, Maria backed her car out of the driveway and slowly drove off.

"How long has he been here?" Jim asked his secretary as he entered his office.

"About an hour I'd say," she answered.

Seated at one of the deputy's desks was Bob Mifflin. The deputy and he were looking through files that were stacked on the desk. Jim watched the proceedings for several minutes through the blinds on his office window before walking back out of his office and across the squad room.

"I see you took me up on my offer," Jim said as he approached the two men at the desk.

Bob looked up at Jim.

"Yeah" the young man began, "I've been asking all over town. Some of the older folks seem to remember some things, but I thought I'd come over here and see if you guys might still have some records from the investigation."

"Why don't we step into my office and we can talk about this further," Jim said signaling his deputy to come along also.

Mifflin got up and followed the sheriff into his office followed by the deputy he had been sitting with before. As they all entered Jim's office, he slowly closed the door.

"Mr. Mifflin, I have a few questions of my own I'd like to ask you if you don't mind."

"Sure," the young man answered.

Jim gestured for the young man to sit and as he himself sat down on the edge of his desk directly in front of Mifflin, he continued, "You're familiar with the murders we've had here over the past week?"

"Yeah, seems to be the talk all over town. I also saw a story this morning in your local paper," Mifflin answered.

"Have you been out to Glenridge Academy since you've been in town?" Jim asked even though he already knew the answer.

The young man looked nervously between Jim and the deputy before speaking.

"Why? What does it matter?"

"When were you there?" Jim continued.

"I was out there on Saturday, but you didn't answer my question," Mifflin asked. "Why are you asking **ME** about that?"

"I'm asking the questions right now young man," Jim answered as he got up and walked around behind his desk.

Looking first at his deputy and then back at the young man, Jim sat down and continued his questioning.

"Why did you lie to me yesterday about being out there?"

The young man sat silent for a moment glancing back and forth between the deputy and Jim.

"It's true isn't it that you've been picked up twice for trouble having to do with women?" Jim asked.

"Oh, now I get it. You think I had something to do with these murders don't you?" The young man said as he got up from his chair. Visibly agitated now he continued, "I told you why I came here. It's not my fault that this happened at the same time. I went out to that campus just to look around, besides, if you didn't know already, I was never charged with anything."

The deputy stepped closer to the young man as Jim pressed on with his questioning.

"Sit down!" he barked, "Why didn't you want me to know you were out there?"

"I had my reasons," Bob replied as the deputy placed his hand on the young mans shoulder directing him to sit back down.

"You know your attitude isn't gonna help you any here with me," Jim said as he sat back down in his own chair.

"How do you expect me to act," Bob said angrily. "I

come in here to try and get some help and the next thing I know, you're accusing me of murder."

"I didn't accuse you of murder young man, I simply asked you some questions," Jim answered.

"Oh well pardon **ME**, but it sure sounds like you're going in that direction," Bob replied abruptly.

"Look Mr. Mifflin," Jim began. "It may well be coincidental that you arrived here at the same time these events started, but I have to look at everything and everyone that might contribute to solving this and right no, you're one of the people I'm looking at. Believe me, If I really had something on you we wouldn't be having this friendly chat. You'd be locked up. Now I would suggest you stay right here in town where I can keep an eye on you, okay?"

"I'm not planning on going anywhere until I find out what happened to my Uncle," Bob answered as he got up and briskly walked out of Jim's office.

"I didn't want to say anything while you were talking to him chief, but his story about his uncle checks out completely," the deputy said as he laid the files he had on to Jim's desk.

Jim stared after the young man as he walked out of the station.

"There's one other thing," the deputy added, "That hooker in Denver? We just found out she was a student at Glenridge. Same year his uncle disappeared."

Jim turned and looked directly at the deputy with one eyebrow raised and a sort of peculiar smirk beginning on his face. He looked back at the front door through which the young man had just exited.

"Now **that's** interesting," he said.

"What are you nuts!" Paul asked as he looked nervously around the cafeteria to see if anyone had heard him. "There's no way we're going back in there tonight."

"It's the perfect spot," Liz insisted. "Nobody's gonna know we're there and we can spend the whole night."

"Did you completely forget the other night?" Paul said.

"No I didn't, but it was probably just he janitor trying to scare us," she reasoned as she slid her hand up Paul's thigh under the table.

As she reached even further she looked longingly into his eyes, though clearly exaggerated, squeezed a bit, and whined softly, "You don't want me to give it to someone else do you?"

Paul looked straight at Liz in disbelief. He'd never met another girl that was so obsessed with having sex all the time. Regardless of the consequences, Liz always seemed to be ready and willing.

"What about the new curfew?" he asked.

"I promise, I'll have you in bed early," she giggled.

Paul rolled his eyes and half smiled. What was he going to do he thought; half the guys on campus would give there right arm to be in his position right now.

Liz got up from the table and gave him a kiss on the check.

"See you there at 9:30," she said as she turned and walked across the cafeteria.

Chapter Six

"Mind if I come in?"

Jim looked up and saw Emily peering in the partially opened door of his office.

"Come on in, the waters fine," he called out as he got up from his desk and met her halfway across the room.

They kissed and separated, she walked to the chair in front of Jim's desk and he went over to the small refrigerator he kept in his office.

"Want something cold to drink?" He asked gazing into the fridge.

"Thanks," came her reply.

Jim reached inside and pulled out two bottled waters and turned and handed her one.

"And to what do I owe this pleasant surprise?" he asked as he sat back down at his desk.

"I had to pick up some research material at the library, so I figured I'd stop by and say hi," Emily answered, "Gotten anything new on those girls' deaths?" she added.

"No, in fact one of my potential suspects really doesn't figure into it at all now," Jim said in a somewhat disgusted tone. "As you can see, I'm up to my ears in call-in leads and conjectures from all over," Jim said gesturing to the piles of papers on his desk.

The door opened and one of his deputy's poked his head in and said,

"Chief, we're ready when you are,"

"Okay, let's go," Jim answered waving he and the other

deputy's into his office for an update on their progress. Emily picked up her drink and her purse to leave when Jim gestured for her to stay.

"No, you stay," he said, "we could use a fresh viewpoint on this."

Four deputies poured into Jim's office and positioned themselves around the room. Each of them said their hellos to Emily and then turned back toward Jim.

"Well? What have we got so far?" Jim asked.

One of the men began, "Joel and I combed that campus all day yesterday and this morning. For as brutal as these murders were, there isn't a trace of evidence anywhere. No fingerprints, no footprints, no hairs, nothing. It's as if this guy is invisible except that some of those kids thought they saw something. With as much blood loss as there is at both crimes scenes, you'd think there would be some kind of blood trail leading off in one direction or another." Turning to Emily, he continued apologetically "I'm sorry ma'am, I didn't mean to be so graphic."

"It's okay," she answered smiling, "Being married to a cop all these years means I get to hear about lots of this kind of stuff."

"What do we have on the Patrick's boy?" Jim asked.

"Every state agency has an APB out on his truck," another deputy began. "The Tucson police have units watching his parents' house twenty-four hours a day. So far nothing, but his roommate told us Saturday that there are clothes and things missing from the room, so it does appear that he ran after the second girls death."

Another deputy interjected his thoughts, "After the first girl and the horrific way she was murdered, why stick around another twenty-four hours to kill yet another girl that he didn't even know?"

The room was silent momentarily as all gave the query some thought. Finally another deputy spoke.

"Maybe to make us think that there **is** a serial killer and throw suspicion off of him?"

- 50 -

"Then why leave at all?" Jim asked.

"And why is he so sadistic with these girls?" a deputy asked.

Jim rustled through the papers on his desk and produced the notes he had made from his conversation with Judith Lansbury in L.A.

"Our killer could be harboring deep seated contempt for young women who, how shall I put it…exhibit a overwhelming zeal for pleasures of the flesh?"

"Eloquently put," Emily laughed as a couple of the deputy's actually looked a little confused and embarrassed.

"In other words he hates horny girls," one of the deputy's translated.

"Exactly," Jim noted, "however everything we've got on this kid so far doesn't even begin to indicate that he has any emotional problems. His parents and neighbors back in Tucson paint a picture of a very well balanced guy. His teachers and coach seem to think he's the last person anyone should suspect, but you never know."

"Maybe he's one of those duel personality types boss, you know like that Jekyll and Hyde story," one of the deputy's offered.

Another of the men took his clipboard and tapped the deputy who had just spoken, sharply on the head.

"What are you guys, the three stooges?" Jim asked.

"Sorry boss," the two answered in unison.

Another of the deputies walked over to the file cabinet and laying his notes down on the top of it interjected.

"You know Chief, that guy Bob Mifflin, well, his story seems to check out everyway we go at it. We talked to quite a few of his friends back home and they all say that he was planning this trip for some time with the express purpose of looking for information about his uncle's disappearance. He's been all over town asking questions and he was even in here. For a possible suspect, he's not very low profile."

Jim had to agree, but right now he was more interested in the expression Emily had gotten on her face when the deputy mentioned Bob Mifflin's name. Directing his attention towards her he asked,

"What is it M?"

Surprised by his question, Emily answered.

"Oh nothing, nothing to do with this. I just remembered something that happened earlier. I'll tell you later."

Jim returned his attention to the deputies assembled in his office.

"Well, we've got two dead girls, one maybe two suspects, no clues and a mayor who wants me to clean this up so as not to scare away tourists. I'd say we've got our work cut out for us boys."

They all nodded in agreement and began to exit single file out of Jim's office. Turning his attention back to his wife he readdressed his question to Emily.

"Well?"

"I think you're going to have a tough week."

Jim stretched back in his chair. Emily got up and walked around the desk. She leaned over and kissed him on the forehead.

"I'll see you at home," she said resignedly knowing that her husband would be immersed in this case until it was solved. It was just his way. As she was about to exit, Jim called after her.

"By the way, what was that you were referring to before?" gesturing to the chair where she had been sitting.

Emily stopped and stepping back into the office she answered.

"Oh probably nothing. This morning Jill, Maria and I were having coffee on my break. When I mentioned the boys name and that he was here looking for information about his uncle, I thought Maria was going to faint right there. She got real pale and ran off to the restroom. When I went in after her to see if she was okay, she was crying and shaking. She didn't look good at all, but she said she was fine and left the restaurant without saying a word. I thought about it more later and thought it was real strange how she reacted when I mentioned that boys' name."

Jim listened intently and then smiling responded.

"Did I ever tell you you'd make a good cop?"

"Do you suppose she knows him?" Emily asked.

"I don't know. Why don't you ask her?" Jim answered.

"That's your job Mr. Sheriff," Emily said laughing as she left his office.

As dusk crept over the countryside, Maria's station wagon hurtled down the deserted wooded road. She didn't know how long she had been driving or even where she was headed. Her mind was filled with so many thoughts that she had developed a headache. She pulled the car over onto the dirt shoulder. The deer in the field next to her seemed to pay her no mind, as they grazed seemingly, not even realizing she existed. Right now, she wished she didn't. Staring out into the woods, Maria slowly reached into the dark zippered bag on the seat next to her. She pulled the black object out and holding it in her hand she let her fingers outline the small caliper pistol. She ran her fingers down the barrel and up again. Slipping her finger into the trigger hole she held it against her chest for several long minutes. She then placed it back inside the bag on the seat next to her and zipped it closed.

"You're home earlier than I expected," Emily said looking up at the late hour on the clock as Jim walked into the kitchen.

"Man can not survive on crime alone," he said in a somber voice as he slipped his hands around her waist from behind. As he pushed her gently against the stove with his hips she turned.

"Now, now, now, dinner first, dessert later."

Jim smiled, turned and walked over to the table in the breakfast nook and sat down. As he looked over the days mail, Emily turned to him.

"I'm a little worried about Maria. I called over there a couple of hours ago and she hadn't come home all day. I told Steve how she wasn't feeling well this morning so he said he was going to call around and see if he could find her. He hasn't called back yet. Do you suppose I should call him back?"

"Maybe she went off the mountain to go shopping?" Jim offered.

"Yeah, well that's possible I guess," Emily answered. "But I would have thought she would tell Steve where she was going."

"Yeah, maybe," Jim answered. "You know yourself she can be a little strange."

Emily knew Jim was right about that. Since she had met Maria she had seen her go through mood swings often. Her friend Jill had known Maria much longer and warned Emily shortly after they had become friends to be aware of Maria's ever changing disposition. According to Jill, there was always something that was bothering Maria very deeply, but she would never reveal what it was to anyone. Not even her husband. She had been known to sometimes just leave for hours at a time and then suddenly re-appear with no explanation. She would say she was just out driving if asked. Today however, she had been gone longer than usual and even Steve was beginning to worry.

"Call over there again and see if he's heard anything," Jim told Emily.

Emily reached for the phone on the wall just as it suddenly rang. The unexpectedness of the timing caught both of them off guard for a moment. Emily grabbed the phone off the wall and raised it to her ear.

"Yes...Hi Steve.... No, I haven't heard a thing, you? Of course I will...yes, he's right here," Emily turned and held out the phone for Jim.

"Hi Steve," Jim said listening. "Yeah no problem. I'll be happy to. Don't worry; I'm sure she's fine. Okay, bye."

Jim hung up the receiver back on the wall.

"Is she still driving that blue Jeep Cherokee?" Jim asked Emily as he picked up the phone again.

She nodded affirmatively. He called the stations and instructed the dispatcher to tell all the deputies to keep an eye open for Maria's Jeep and to call him immediately if they find her. Emily smiled as he hung up the phone.

"Thanks honey," she said.

"Let's eat, I'm starved," Jim said.

The red light on the phone on the dresser was flashing when Bob Mifflin entered the motel room. Someone must have called while he was out he figured. He hoped it wasn't the sheriff. He'd had enough of him for one day. He picked up the jacket he had just thrown on the bed upon entering and decided he would go over to the motel office and retrieve the message personally. He wanted to pick up the local paper they had on the counter there anyway. He left his room and began walking along the veranda that stretched the length of the building. The mountain air had a chill to it and Bob slipped the jacket he had brought on and zipped it up.

As he entered the office and walked over to the counter, he glanced up as the old parliament clock on the wall chimed 11:00 o'clock. The old man behind the counter got up, turned around and spoke.

"There was a woman in here earlier looking for you. She seemed real anxious to see you though. I told her you weren't here."

"Did she say what she wanted? Who she was?" Bob asked the old man.

"I don't know who she was, but I think she's a local. Had a local sticker on her back window. Said she'd be back," the old man answered.

Bob nodded and turned to walk out. He grabbed one of the complimentary newspapers off the counter and walked back out into the chilly night air. As he approached his room he heard the sound of a car door opening. He looked around him but saw no one. Just ahead though, he could barely make out a figure, almost a shadow of a figure between the parked cars. He slowed his pace as he approached the figure. Now he could make out that it was a woman though barely discernable. She wore a scarf over her head and across her face as if to disguise her identity. The overcoat she had on blended so well with the darkness it was difficult to see her completely. He decided he would simply continue to his room and ignore this person, but just as he came adjacent to her she spoke.

"Are you Mr. Mifflin?" the woman asked in a nervously shaky voice.

Bob stopped dead in his tracks. It was at that moment he noticed something in her hand. He couldn't tell exactly what it was but fear suddenly swept over him.

"Look lady, I don't have any money and I don't want any trouble," he said cautiously.

She repeated herself.

"Are you Mr. Mifflin?" she asked with a little more insistence in her voice.

"Yes I am. Can I help you?" he asked.

"Maybe we can help each other," she answered almost whispering.

She came closer from between the cars and into the light. Bob could now see that she was holding a small dark zippered bag. He worried what she might have in that bag.

"Can we go inside where we can talk?" she asked almost apologetically.

"Uh...sure," he answered fumbling with his room key.

He still was very nervous and unsure about what was happening at this point. He walked the few steps more to his room and slipped the key in the lock. As he turned to gesture the woman to join him, he saw that she hadn't moved.

"You really are here just to find out about your uncle aren't you?" she asked.

Suddenly Bob's anxiety level began to drop a few notches as he realized that this was probably not a robbery, as he had originally feared. Bob looked out around the dark parking lot and nodded affirmatively. Obviously the sheriff wasn't the only one who had some doubts about his appearance here in town. He looked back at the woman standing there and gestured for her to come in to his room.

"I'm only here to find out about what happened to my uncle," he sighed.

The woman took the few steps and followed him into the room. Bob closed the door behind them.

Chapter Seven

"Unit Two, communication check," the female voice came across the radio.

"I'm tellin' you man, they're not paying me enough money to get me to walk around this campus tonight. I'm staying right here inside this car," the security guards voice cracked nervously into the two-way radio.

The young girl sitting at the dispatcher's desk at Alpine Security smiled and laughingly answered.

"Josh, has anybody ever told you what a chicken shit you are?"

"Hey! You come out here then," he answered.

"Unit One, communication check," she called out across the radios.

"Unit One, Roger that. All's well here. I just saw one of the sheriff's units drive behind the gym."

"I'll be out of the unit patrolling for ten minutes," a voice answered.

"Roger that Two, be careful," came the reply from the dispatcher.

"Hey Johnson," came a voice from Alpine Unit Two.

"Keep your eyes open. If you see anyone running across the campus with an ax in their hand, be sure and ask them where they're going."

"Very cute Josh. I'll be sure and send them over your way."

"Boys, you want to stop playing on the radio and get serious here?" came a voice over the channel that was also open to the sheriffs units.

"Yes sir," the Alpine units answered in unison.

The security company had been Jim's idea. The chancellor hadn't been to receptive when it was posed to him this morning, but with all that had happened thus far and the demands of the parents for better security it was pretty hard to say no. With the extra bodies on hand, Jim figured whoever was doing this might be less likely to act and maybe even move out of the area.

The young man sitting in the Alpine Security Unit next to the girls dorm watched as another sheriff cruiser went by and disappeared around the building. His own car was hidden in the shadows between the two buildings. As he reached into his pocket for a cigarette, he noticed something in his periphery vision. Behind the girls dorm he detected a distinct movement. He slowly turned his head in that direction straining to see if there had in fact been something moving. At first he didn't see it, but as his eyes focused more on the bushes behind the building he made out a shadow against the brick wall of the girls dorm. It moved only slightly, but enough for him to now know with absolute certainty that something was there.

For a moment he froze. He remembered the grizzly descriptions of the two girls that had been killed already. *What kind of monster could this be* he thought. He felt the fear racing up his spine as he tried to think of what to do next. After all, he wasn't a veteran cop who knew exactly how to handle a situation like this. Suddenly he realized that he was faced with something that was probably more terrifying than anything he could imagine. Should he step out of the car and confront this monster and possibly die trying to apprehend it, or should he remain motionless and quietly call for back up. After all, maybe it didn't see him. Before he could decide, the shadow moved along the wall and into the bushes next to the dorm.

He could now make out that it was a human form and holding something large in it's hand. Suddenly the adrenalin kicked in and he reached for both the spotlight and the two-way radio at the same time. Shining the light directly at the subject he yelled into the handset.

"I'VE GOT IT! IT'S HERE BEHIND THE GIRLS DORM! SOMEBODY, ANYBODY GET ME SOME HELP HERE FAST!"

He threw open the door to his car and as his spotlight shone on the subject. Dropping the two-way onto the front seat, he reached down and drew his service revolver from its holster. Pointing it straight at the figure in the bushes and yelled.

"FREEZE! DON'T YOU MOVE OR I'LL BLOW YOUR HEAD OFF!"

The figure turned and looked straight at him, His own mixture of fear and adrenalin made it impossible for him to tell if the figure was frightened or enraged. He only knew at that moment he had to keep it from going anywhere. He shouted.

"GET OUT OF THOSE BUSHES AND GET DOWN ON THE GROUND FACE DOWN! DO IT! RIGHT NOW!"

The figure stepped slowly away from the bushes but didn't get down as commanded. The security guard stepped around the car door and took two steps. He could now see that the figure was holding a large piece of iron, possibly a large crowbar. He yelled further commands.

"DROP WHAT YOU'RE HOLDING OR I SWEAR TO GOD I'LL SHOOT YOU!"

It seemed like an eternity but in only a matter of moments several sheriffs' cruisers came screaming around the building. Their light bars flashing, they bounced up over the curb and across the grass and came sliding to a stop directly facing the frozen figure before them. Leaping from their cars, their weapons already drawn, they too shouted at the figure to drop what he was holding and get down on the ground. There seemed to be utter confusion as they all yelled commands at the figure. Even the security guard felt intimidated as the deputies moved in closer to the person, now finally dropping what he was holding and getting down on the ground. As one deputy continued pointing his shotgun at the figure on the ground, another knelt down next to him, placing his knee on the back of the man's neck and grabbing one of his arms. He slapped handcuffs on one wrist as another deputy pulled his other arm around in back of his body and clasped the other wrist into the handcuffs. As the two officers stood up the second story door on the girls dorm flew open and several girls came rushing out to see what was going on.

"**GET BACK INSIDE!**" the deputy barked and the girls quickly ran back inside slamming the door behind them.

"Turn over and stand up slowly," a deputy instructed the suspect.

Another deputy picked up what was now clearly visible as a very large crowbar.

"I'll bet you can do a lot of damage with this baby eh?" the deputy said holding the crowbar up in the face of the subject.

The suspect, now standing looked frightened and unsure of what was going on.

The security guard stepped in a little closer now feeling much safer now that real law enforcement had things under control. He had never seen a real life killer before and he was excited to be a part of this whole scene. He saw in the light of the cruisers that the suspect was actually a very young man. Maybe even a student here at Glenridge he thought.

"You can put your gun away now," one of the deputies said to him as he put his hand on the still shaking security guards hand.

Embarrassed, he lowered his pistol and secured it in the holster.

"We've got this now, you security people can withdraw some," the deputy instructed him.

Still shaking a little, the security guard walked back to his car.

"What's your name?" one deputy asked the suspect.

The young man was shaking and appeared to want to cry.

"Paul Esterhaus," he answered in a tremulous voice.

"Are you a student here?" the deputy asked.

"Yes sir," the boy answered, his voice cracking with fear.

"Did you really think you were gonna get away with another one?" the deputy asked incredulously.

"I'm not the killer. I was just going to meet a girl," he answered.

"With a crowbar!" another deputy shouted.

"It was for the back door," the boy answered timidly.

"What back door?" the deputy asked.

"Over there," the boy gestured as best he could. "It's got a bunch of stuff blocking it and it's really hard to open."

The deputies looked over at where the boy had gestured. They were looking at the old brick structure that was the main administrative building just several yards across the lawn from the girls dorm. They all returned looking at the boy handcuffed before them. Two more sheriffs cars pulled up between the buildings and several more deputies emerged.

"Is this our guy?" one of them shouted as they all approached.

"Anybody call the chief?" another deputy asked.

"I called him as soon as I heard the security guy calling for help," a deputy answered.

As the deputies that had just arrived passed the security guard, now standing next to his car, one of them commented.

"You did good work son," administering a congratulatory slap on his back.

"So what's this guys story?" asked one of the newly arrived deputies.

"Claims he's a student here and he was just going to meet a girl over at the main building. The crowbar was to open the back door," the deputy standing directly in front of the young man answered.

The tone in the deputies voice made it clear to the young man in handcuffs that they weren't really buying his story.

"Honest, I swear, I really was meeting a girl. We were going in there to fool around," the young man pleaded.

"Let's get him in the car," one of the deputies said.

Two deputies placed their hands under the boy's arms to guide him to one of the sheriff cars. Suddenly they all stopped cold.

"What was that?" one of the deputies asked.

Suddenly there was a terrifying howling. Everyone stopped and listened intently.

"What the hell was that?" one of the deputies asked. There it was again. The most horrifying sound any of them had ever heard. It seemed to be coming from the top floor of the administration building. It was non-stop now but mixed with it was a scream. A female scream, a blood curdling scream.

"What the hell is going on up there?" A deputy shouted.

The young handcuffed man broke free of the two deputies whose attention was now on what they were hearing from up above and rushed a few steps towards the old building.

"Liz!" he shouted. "That's the girl I was supposed to meet!"

"Stay with him," one of the deputies directed to the security guard and drawing their weapons they all rushed towards the old building that now was harboring the most horrible sounds imaginable.

Besides the ungodly howling was the very clear sound of a female screaming.

"Cover every exit! I don't want this bastard getting away from us," the senior deputy shouted as they all worked their way around the building.

Suddenly a window shattered from above them. Two of the deputies that were coming around that side of the building felt the glass falling on them. It was however the deep thump they heard that hit the ground next to them that caused them to freeze in their tracks. They splayed their flashlights across the lawn to see what might have fallen. The howling had stopped, but the screaming was still continuing.

"Oh my God!" one of them shouted as he turned and vomited.

The other deputy turned his light towards where his partner had been shining his to see what had caused him to react that way. There lying on the ground before him was the bloodied stump of an arm. Ripped from its socket, blood pouring from its open end. It lay there quivering for a moment, the fingers still moving. All around the building, the deputies continued, breaking windows and breaking down doors, whatever they could to gain entry into the building. As they converged in the main hallway, they could hear the horrifying screaming of the young girl presumed to be up there.

Whatever unspeakable horror she was suffering, it seemed unlikely they would be able to get to her in time. As several deputies bounded up the huge stairway towards the second floor and beyond, they were repelled by an overpowering odor that literally caused them to fall back several steps. It seemed to sweep down the stairwell from above them like a strong wind. It seemed as if a noxious gas had been released to hold anyone back from ascending the staircase. It smelled like death itself. Pulling their shirt tails out and covering their noses the deputies leaped up the stairs to where the screaming seemed to be coming from. Suddenly the only sounds in the building were the sound of the deputy's boots on the stairs as the clamored upward. The howling had stopped as well as the horrible screaming. The odor they had been experiencing also disappeared as suddenly as it had come.

The deputies stopped and stood quietly for a moment hoping to hear in what direction the assailant might be moving. Realizing that the crime had already been committed and that the killer would now be making his escape, they readied themselves for wherever he might appear. Weapons drawn and pointing, they now slowly crept up the stairs. As they finally reached the attic door without having encountered anyone, a sense of overwhelming dread came over the men who were now there. Since they had not seen anyone, it seemed likely that the killer was still in the attic. What form of homicidal maniac might they encounter inside. How horrifying a scene were they going to find behind this door.

"We've got to get some light up here," one of them whispered. "Once we get that door open it's gonna be pitch black in there."

They stood with their backs to the wall listening for any sound at all from beyond the door. Two more deputies arrived. They had large spotlights with them. One of them nearly whispering, spoke into his radio.

"We're outside the attic. We've got a couple of spotlights. We're going in."

A voice came back over the radio.

"Wait a minute, we're getting the lights on in the building. We've got every exit covered. He's not getting out of here without somebody seeing him. Chief just pulled up, hold on for a moment."

The deputies waited momentarily. They concurred that they couldn't wait any longer. Suddenly the lights went on in the entire building. It shone up the staircase but they didn't know if there were any lights on in the attic. They looked down at the base of the door. No light appeared. They had to go in.

Chapter Eight

Bob Mifflin sat Indian style on the bed looking across the motel room at he woman who had approached him outside. She sat at the table by the window staring at the wall as though a million miles away. He could see tears welling up in her eyes. Neither of them had spoken since entering the room; he not knowing what to say and she apparently not knowing where to begin. Finally the silence was broken as the woman spoke.

"I knew your uncle...well, sort of," she began almost in tears. "There were a bunch of us girls...a club like. I don't know how I got involved. I really didn't want to be in the club, but I was. Cathy, that was my best friend back then, she made me. We really didn't do any harm. I was very confused back then and she said she'd tell everyone about me if I didn't go along. Anyway, it seemed harmless. They would see how many boys they could have sex with each month. It was a game to them. They even had a scoring system. Anyway, there was this one boy who was kind of quiet. Kept to himself mostly, didn't seem like he was a player you might say. The girls decided they wanted to introduce him to a wilder side of life. Cathy made like she was real interested in him and convinced him he should join her one Sunday for some fun. He didn't know we all would be there. He was your uncle..."

The woman spoke and remembered the events of the past.

Sunday April 12th, 1965.

It was raining lightly as those students who wanted to go to morning services, were scurrying across the campus to the little church. Cathy and Lisa were huddled beneath the great wooden staircase in the main administration building that led all the way up to the attic.

"Are you sure nobody else is gonna be in here?" Lisa asked.

"Don't worry, the coast is clear. I made a deal with Ray," Cathy answered.

"The janitor?" Lisa said incredulously.

"Yeah, he and I have an understanding you might say," Cathy giggled.

"Where's Maria? She said she'd come. She's such a chicken," Lisa said.

"She'll be along," Cathy whispered confidently.

"What is it with you two. She never wants to do this with us but somehow you always manage to get her to come along," Lisa added.

"Shhh," Cathy whispered as they heard the heavy wood door across the hallway open.

"Oh shit," Lisa muttered. "I thought you said nobody was gonna be here today. What are we gonna do?"

"Relax silly, it's probably him. He came in the same way we did," Cathy said.

As the figure came around the corner and stopped in front of the two girls, Lisa let out an audible sigh of relief.

"I got lost," the young man said sheepishly.

"Nobody saw you did they?" Cathy asked.

"Who is this?" he asked, looking at Lisa.

Stepping up next to Lisa, Cathy responded.

"John Mifflin, I'd like you to meet one of my friends Lisa Dunbar. Lisa, this is John."

"I thought I was just meeting you here," John said to Cathy a little surprised.

"Well I thought I'd bring along a couple of friends. You don't mind do you?" she said giggling.

"A couple of friends?" John asked just as the heavy door across the hallway opened again.

They all turned their heads as Maria scurried across the darkened hallway to where they were all standing.

"What took you so long?" Lisa asked as they all came around the banister and started climbing the stairs.

"I didn't know what to wear," Maria answered timidly.

Cathy and Lisa giggled at the obvious flaw in Maria's concern. As they finally reached the attic door, A feeling of excitement ran through them as Lisa reached for the doorknob.

"It's locked," she said surprised although she knew it would be.

No one was ever allowed up here. Cathy reached in her pocket and produced a key and displayed to everyone.

"How did you get that?" Lisa squealed.

"I told you, Ray and I have an understanding," she said coyly as she reached over and slipped the key into the lock.

Lisa and Maria looked at each other and giggled in unison, "The Janitor?"

Once inside, Cathy led the party across the room and around a partition where on the floor laid an old mattress, suitable for nothing more than what they all had planned for this afternoon.

"We're all gonna do this together?" John asked in amazement.

"You can have it any way you want," Lisa purred as she sat down on the edge of the mattress and began untying her tennis shoes.

Maria stepped back against the wall, embarrassed by the moment. Since she had been compelled to accompany Cathy and Lisa on a few of their conquests, she had found that she did in fact enjoy the sex, but it still bothered her terribly that some of the boys were forced to do things they didn't always seem willing to do.

"Come on Maria, don't be a wall flower again," Cathy

called out as she began unbuttoning her blouse. "Get over here."

Maria's eyes met John's for a moment. She felt as though he sensed that she really didn't want to be there, but understood.

"Don't be shy, lay down. We won't bite," Cathy cooed as she circled the mattress slipping off her blouse as she walked.

John's eyes were fixed upon her very large breasts as they swung slowly with the rhythm of each step. He smiled broadly and stepped towards the mattress. As Lisa lifted her legs and slipped her shorts down around her ankles, she added.

"We won't bite too much anyway."

Maria watched as the two girls undressed John and flung all their clothes across a pile of unused bricks stacked nearby.

They had him on his back in seconds and began performing all sorts of erotic pleasures on him. At first he tried to be gentlemanly with them, but as the first hour turned into the second, the girls became more and more demanding of his body until finally he could only lay there on the mattress as they took their turns on his sweating and weakening body.

"Get in here Maria, stop simply touching and get involved," Cathy ordered.

"Let her be Cathy, maybe she doesn't like this one," Lisa said as she raised her head.

"Are you waiting for me sweetheart?" Cathy said to Maria teasingly.

Maria squinted her eyes and looked sternly at Cathy as though she had said something she shouldn't have. Even though she had wanted to remain out of the goings on, the sight of it all had aroused her to the point she had removed all her clothing. She moved over the mattress as Lisa took her hand and guided her atop the tiring boy beneath them.

John pleaded that they might stop for a while so that he could gather some strength back, but Cathy just laughed and proceeded with what she was doing.

Eventually John was begging for them all to stop. His body ached and he was so exhausted from the workout these girls were giving him.

"You're not going anywhere until we say," Cathy said threateningly. "We're just getting warmed up."

John looked up at Maria who looked away at Cathy. Lisa and Cathy had tied Johns ankles and wrists to posts around the mattress leaving him basically spread eagle for them to satisfy their lust filled games. It seemed as though yet another hour had passed before the three girls paused.

The boy on the sweat soaked mattress was so weak and tired he could barely move. His throat was parched as he tried to speak begging the girls to set him free.

Cathy untied him and Maria gave him a drink from her now warm water bottle. John said nothing as he tried to get up but fell backwards from his weakened legs.

"I think he's ready for more," Lisa laughingly said.

"No, No really girls. I need a break," John insisted as he tried again unsuccessfully to get up off the mattress.

Maria moved away from John to give more room for him to attempt to get to his feet. Cathy reached out and grabbed his arm as if to pull him back down to her.

"You HAVE to give me a break," he insisted as he pulled his arm away.

Cathy and Lisa just laughed wearily. Lisa reached to grab his arm this time. John knew he had to break free from these girls. This was crazy he thought, they weren't going to stop. With all the strength he could muster, he pushed himself up from the mattress. His legs were so weak and shaky it felt as though they would buckle right out from under him. The sudden rise from the mattress and his weakened state made him suddenly feel very dizzy. He felt himself losing his balance and falling backwards to the floor he passed out. Everything went white.

"Oh my God!" Lisa screamed "He's unconscious."

"He hit his head on those bricks" Maria cried out as she crawled over to his motionless body.

Cathy rose to her knees and crawled over to where John lay still. A small dark puddle now slowly began to appear under his head. It grew in size rapidly.

"Is he dead?" Lisa whispered.

"Nah, he's just knocked, he'll be fine," Cathy answered although she sounded a little unsure of herself.

Lisa reached over and lifted his arm and pressed her thumb against his wrist. She looked over at Cathy and began crying. Maria began to cry as well. The dark puddle under his head had now grown considerably and Lisa moved back away from it.

"My God, what have we done! He's dead." she cried out.

"We didn't do this. It was an accident. We have to stay calm, it was an accident," Cathy argued seemingly trying to convince herself as much as the others.

The three girls stood up and staring down at the body before them cried.

"What are we going to do!" Maria cried.

"I can't believe this is happening," Cathy said in a much calmer voice now.

She began pacing back and forth in front of the lifeless form on the attic floor.

"We're all going to hell for this one," Lisa said quietly.

"How are we ever going to explain this?" Maria cried as she wiped the tears from her face. "We'll be kicked out of school. We'll probably all go to jail."

"We've gotta stay calm. We can't panic," Cathy assured them. "I'll figure something out. Whatever we do, we have to stick together on this. No matter what," she went on.

Cathy sat back down on the mattress, drawing her knees up to her chest and began slowly rocking back and forth as she thought.

Several minutes passed when she finally spoke.

"We've got to stick together."

"…and that's exactly what we did," Maria said softly sobbing. "As crazy as it was, we did the most unbelievable thing. We made a pact, right there and then, a solemn oath that we would never speak a word of what happened up there to anyone as long as we lived. And then we buried him, right there in the wall. There were a couple of bags of cement and Lisa went and got a large bucket of water. We put him in a nook in the wall and used the bricks that were left there to cover him up. Lisa and I were seniors so we graduated that year. Cathy was only a junior but she dropped out of school shortly after the incident and was never heard from again. Lisa moved away, but I stayed here living with this nightmare all these years. I never even told my husband. Only one other person knew what happened."

Maria broke down crying uncontrollably and covered her face with her hands. For several minutes Bob could say nothing. Whether it was shock or just plain disbelief, he couldn't find any words that would fit to respond to this astounding story he had just been told. Finally, Maria lifted her head and spoke again.

"First I heard that Lisa went crazy and was working as a hooker somewhere. Then Cathy's life deteriorated into drugs and alcohol and finally she was murdered. I thought I would be next. Then you showed up here and those girls started dying, I was frightened. I wasn't sure what was going on. I only knew that I couldn't live with this any longer."

Bob sat quietly on the bed thinking that he should have a million questions right now, but none came to mind.

"I had actually thought about killing myself earlier today," Maria said as she slowly drew the zipper on the bag she had brought in the room with her.

"Then I thought," she added. "If I came here and talked to you, and you were the killer, I could kill you."

She slowly drew the pistol out of the bag and held it so Bob could clearly see it. He said nothing but a cold shiver of fear shot through his body. Would he die right here because of the ghosts that haunted this lady?

"I don't think you're the killer though," Maria said as she slipped the pistol back inside the bag and very slowly zipped it back up.

Bob released a barely audible sigh of relief.

"Who do you think it might be?" he asked Maria.

"The one person who hates us the most," she replied wearily.

Bob thought about her answer for a long time, but dismissed it as the ramblings of a woman whose mental state was probably weakened anyway. She hung her head and wept silently. Bob slowly got up and sitting down next to her on the bed, he put his arm over her shoulder and spoke.

"I don't think you'll need to worry about this too much longer. The sheriff seems to be pretty good at doing his job."

The wood splintered easily because of it's age as the men kicked in the door. As it crashed open the deputies piled through, each with their weapon drawn. As more and more floodlights were brought into the attic, they exposed the horror that had gone on in there only moments before. It appeared as though gallons of red paint had exploded and splattered everywhere. The floor was so covered that two deputies slipped and fell in it. The men moved cautiously across the room in case the killer was hiding behind something.

"Be careful boys, I think this floor is shot," one of the deputies called out as his foot broke through a floorboard.

"We're inside," another of the deputies whispered into his radio.

Jim Fremont could be heard answering as he ascended the stairs.

"We're right behind you. Find anything yet?"

"Negative boss, just a whole lot of blood," came the answer.

"Oh God," one of the deputies uttered as he rounded a corner.

Several more men immediately joined him. A couple turned back in revulsion.

It was hard to believe what they saw. There sprawled out spread eagle on what appeared to be an old rotted mattress were the remains of a young girl. Her body had been ripped apart even more grotesquely than the others. Her lower abdomen to her legs had been completely ripped out and her insides strewn across the floor beneath her. One arm was completely gone and one of her legs was lying four feet away from her. The expression on her face was of utter and indescribable horror. Whatever she had seen had been so terrifying that it left her hair completely white and her eye bulging nearly out of their sockets.

Jim Fremont came up behind the deputies and parted them as he made his way to the scene. He surveyed the grizzly remains and then turning to his men asked.

"So where is he?"

"He's not here. Nobody's here," one of them answered.

"Well where the hell did he go? He didn't just fly away did he? Look for a trap door or something," Jim barked.

The many men in the attic at this point spread out and began looking everywhere, turning things over and pushing things aside while keeping clear of the actual crime scene.

Jim spoke into his radio to the deputies that were surrounding the building.

"Anyone out there see anything?"

"No boss, nothing moving out here. He hasn't come out of the building," came the reply.

"I want a floor by floor, room by room search of this entire building. Stay in pairs and be alert," Jim ordered.

"Boss, what is that smell in here?" one of the deputies asked.

Jim had noticed the obnoxious odor while he was ascending the stairs before they broke into the attic. He remembered that an odor had been mentioned in conjunction with several interviews that had been taken. Now he figured it had to have a connection here with the murderer.

"Hold up guys, before you go let's see if we can find where that smell is coming from," Jim said to his men.

He, along with the other deputies started moving slowly around the attic again like bloodhounds sniffing out their prey.

"Boss, over here," one of the men called out near the body of the girl. "It seems to be stronger over here," he said as he stood by one of the old exterior walls.

Jim looked around and saw nothing at first. Then he noticed two bricks that were on the floor. They appeared to have been knocked loose from the wall in front of him. He reached down and placed his nose closer to the opening.

"Whew!" he drew back abruptly. "It's coming from in there alright."

Jim stepped back and surveyed the wall. After a moment or two he turned and said;

"Couple of you guys get some crowbars or a pick ax and break these bricks away from there."

"Boss, you don't really think he snuck away into that tiny little hole now do you?" one of the deputies asked incredulously.

Jim heard a few snickers from behind him.

"Just do it!" he barked back.

He himself wasn't sure why he wanted it done but he felt that the smell in that wall was going to have something to do with these murders. In a few moments, a couple of his men had returned with some crowbars and began breaking away the bricks on the wall. As they worked, Jim noticed that it appeared as though there were a cavity behind the brick wall. As the men continued, Mr. Thompson, the Chancellor arrived at the door to the attic.

"I'm sorry I couldn't get here any sooner to turn on the lights," he apologized. No one has been up here in over twenty years or more. Be careful, the flooring is supposed to be bad."

"We had to break in. We couldn't wait," one of the deputies told him.

"How'd he get in here?" Jim asked as he instructed one

- 75 -

of his deputies to escort Thompson out of the building as this was still an active crime scene with a suspect possibly still inside.

"Okay, some of you go ahead now and begin that search. Remember, every inch of this building," Jim instructed. "He's gotta be in here somewhere."

Several of his men left to carry out the order while the dismantling of the brick wall continued. Jim turned his attention to the young girl's dismembered body laying next to him. He walked carefully around the mattress stepping over and around the blood spattered floor. There had to be blood trailing outside this room he thought even though that had not been the case in the last two killings. With such carnage, the killer would have to be covered in blood. The two men chipping away at the wall suddenly stopped.

"He Chief, look at this," one of them called out.

Jim gingerly stepped around the mattress once again and over to the enlarged cavity now exposed inside the wall. There, laying in an almost fetal position were the skeletal remains of a human. The men covered their noses with their hands as the stench of the decomposed body increased into the air.

"Well our killer didn't come in here. This space was already taken," the deputy offered sarcastically.

"Who do you suppose it is?" another deputy asked.

Jim stepped back and looked again at the girl's body on the mattress.

"This has been a busy attic," he said.

He walked back over to the wall and peered inside the cavity at the skeletal remains.

"Let's secure this building and get the M.E. up here," he ordered.

Almost an hour had already passed and Jim was pretty certain that whoever had killed this girl had somehow slipped out of the building undetected while they were all scrambling to get in. How though was the question? Whoever this was, he was as elusive as a wisp of smoke with a real bad case of body odor. Jim fingered the button on his radio and called out to one of his other officers.

"Fred, you there, this is mobile one. Are you still with our boy out there?"

A few moments passed and then a voice crackled over the two-way in response.

"That's affirmative chief. He's been in his room all evening."

"Are you sure he's in there?" Jim called back.

"Yeah boss, I'm sure. He even had a lady friend in there with him for quite awhile," came the reply.

"Well, pick him up and bring him back to the station," Jim ordered.

"Roger that chief," the officer on the other end of the radio answered.

Jim left the attic and made his way down the stairs to the main entrance.

The building and the surrounding grounds were filled with deputies and security personnel. The entire perimeter of the building was entwined in yellow crime scene tape. Jim stepped out into the cool night air. Thompson and several deputies were standing on the steps.

"Who has keys to that attic?" Jim asked Thompson.

"To be honest with you, I have no idea where they are. Since the room was considered unsafe so many years ago, nobody goes up there. It's possible the janitor might know where they are," Thompson replied.

"Well, that room was locked from the inside when my deputies tried to gain access, but that girl got in someway," Jim answered clearly unsatisfied with the response he had drawn thus far.

He walked down the steps and around the building where the young man had been detained earlier. As he approached, he saw that the boy was crying.

"What's his story?" Jim asked.

"Says he was gonna meet the girl up there so they could fool around," the deputy answered.

"Does he know how she was going to get into the attic?" Jim asked.

The deputy shrugged not knowing.

"Excuse me young man, I'm Sheriff Fremont. Mind if I ask you a few more questions?"

The boy looked up and wiped the tears from his face with his still handcuffed hands.

"Somebody take these off of him" Jim ordered referring to the restraints on the boy's wrists.

A deputy stepped up and unlocked the handcuffs.

"Can you tell me how your girlfriend was going to get into the attic?" Jim asked politely.

"I don't know sir; you see she wasn't really my girlfriend. We just met a couple of weeks ago. She came on real strong like she really wanted me, ya know?" The boy said. "We started last week and she said she wanted to do it up there. I told her nobody was allowed up there and especially now with all this going on. I knew we should have never gone back in there."

"What do you mean...gone back," Jim asked curiously.

"Were you guys in that attic before?"

"No sir. We got scared out of there last night," the boy replied.

"Who scared you out?" Jim asked curiously.

He was getting more curious as he wondered if the killer had been in the building yesterday.

"We didn't know. We thought it might have been the janitor but whoever it was, they let off some serious stink bombs or something," the boy answered.

"Stink bombs?" Jim asked.

"It must have been," the young man continued. "He made the whole hallway smell real bad. Anyway, we got the heck out of there real quick. I didn't want to go back, but Liz insisted. If only I had stopped her," he said sadly as he looked up at the broken window above.

"I may have some more questions for you in the morning," Jim said as he handed him off to one of his

- 78 -

deputies. "Take him back to his dorm."

Jim turned and looked over at the side of the building as two of his men were placing the blood soaked arm into a plastic bag. Another of his men walked up beside him and spoke.

"So far Chief we've found absolutely nothing. Nada. Zip. This guy disappeared right out from under us. There isn't a trace. I don't know how he did it."

Jim stood looking at the old massive building for a long time. As he turned and walked back around to the front steps, Fred pulled up with Bob Mifflin in the back of his patrol car. Jim walked directly down to the waiting car and opened the back door and stuck his head in.

"I hear you found my uncle," Bob said immediately. Raising an eyebrow, Jim responded.

"What makes you think it's your uncle?"

He was astonished that Bob even knew already about the surprising discovery they had found in the wall of the attic.

"Your deputy mentioned on the way over that you guys had found something else up there in the attic," Bob replied.

"Yeah, but I didn't tell you it was a body," the deputy driving interjected.

"How do you know it's your uncle?" Jim asked again only this time with a bit more impatience.

"You found him in the wall didn't you?" Bob asked.

Jim stared at the young man seated in the back seat and then turning to his deputy behind the wheel he said abruptly;

"Take him down to the office. I'll be along shortly."

Jim slammed the car door shut and the car sped away. Jim turned and looked back at the large brick edifice looming before him. Everything seemed surreal as he watched his men scurrying in and out and around the building. Nothing made any sense. He walked up the steps and back inside.

Chapter Nine

It was hours before Jim walked back into his office. He slammed the door shut behind him. Seated in front of his desk was Bob Mifflin. Around the room were three of his deputies seemingly standing guard.

"First of all, I want to apologize for making you wait so long and for being so abrupt with you out there," Jim said as he sat down at his desk and gestured to the deputies that they could leave. "These killings have gotten me very frustrated. Well. Obviously you're not our killer unless you've figured out how to be in two places at the same time," he continued. "I am curious however how you came to be so sure that's your uncle we found up there."

"I can't tell you how I found out. I made a promise that I'd like to keep, but I think once you've checked out the remains, you'll find out it's my uncle," Bob answered.

"I'm having the bones removed and taken to the Medical Examiners office now," Jim said. "Mark is pretty good at this stuff so he should be able to give us an answer pretty soon. He may have to send something out for analysis but it shouldn't take too long. In the meantime, I told him you would help him with any information he might need."

"Of course," Bob answered. "You know sir; I have this theory about your murders here. It's pretty weird, but it might...."

Before Bob could continue, the door to Jim's office flew open and a deputy barged in.

"Sorry to bother you boss but I thought you'd want to

know. I've got Utah Highway Patrol on the line. They just picked up Tim Patricks on Interstate 80 just outside of Salt Lake City headed this way."

Jim thought that this might be the break he was hoping for. His only other strong suspect had just been picked up over 500 miles away. This case certainly wasn't getting any easier.

"I'm sorry Mr. Mifflin but I've got to take this call," he apologized as he reached for the phone. "Perhaps we can talk again tomorrow."

Bob got up and walked out of the office.

"You look like you've been run over by a Mack truck," Emily said as Jim walked in the kitchen door.

"It's been a long day," he answered exhausted.

He had only been able to grab an hour of sleep after finishing up out at the academy and then following up on the information about the boy they had picked up in Utah.

"I hear you got the kid that disappeared?" Emily said.

"Yeah, a whole lot of good it did. They faxed his statement to me this morning. Apparently he was with the Jennings girl that night but when she left to shower and didn't return after a while, he figured she met up with a girlfriend or something so he just grabbed his clothes and left. Then he grabbed his ski's and took off for a weekend of late spring skiing. His alibi is as solid as stone too. Everybody that saw him or was with him up there checks out also. He was just pulling out of Salt Lake when this last girl got it. Then this afternoon, Mark got the dental records of that missing kid back in '65 delivered by courier. They're a perfect match as well as the other evidence he gathered. Seems those bones really are that guy Mifflin's uncle. He's taking him home to bury the remains in the morning."

"What about all that trouble he'd been in before? Was there any connection?" Emily asked.

"Apparently when he was picked up in Denver," Jim

began, "He had found out that his old girlfriend's mother had gone to school here back around the time his uncle did. He was trying to find out if she knew his uncle. It was a case of wrong place at the wrong time. He arrived just as she got murdered so they hauled him in. Had to let him go though since they couldn't really get any evidence on him. Now the Mayor is all over my ass because we're back to square one with NO suspects and two more news crews showed up in front of my office as I was leaving just now. Oh yeah," he continued. "And then there's that crazy old psychic gypsy or whatever she is from out in the woods? She came into town and was telling Brett over at the paper that there won't be anymore murders here. She says I solved them all last night. Cute eh?"

"Maria's home," Emily said cheerfully as she took Jim in her arms.

"Well I'm glad to hear something ended well last night," Jim answered.

Four months have passed up there in the mountains. There actually weren't any more murders, and Glenridge Academy returned to normalcy. The main building restoration was completed and the historical marker was placed prominently on the entrance.

School has been out a while and only the landscaping crews are out there keeping the place clean for next semester. The news crews are all gone and even tourism picked back up much to the Mayors delight. Sheriff Jim Fremont however, is still grappling with the mystery of three unsolved brutal murders with absolutely no suspects. One woman in this small Sierra town thinks she knows, but she's not telling.

THE END

Tales from the Mind Field

GOING HOME
By
R.M.VILLORIA

Chapter One

Still falling, Emma reached for anything to grab hold of but, her hand kept slipping off everything she passed. The pain, as her knuckles smashed against the obstacles in the dark, seemed to rip her will to fight back more and more as she descended further and further into this abominable abyss. Her screams seemed silent, yet she knew she was screaming at the top of her lungs. Why couldn't anybody hear her? Why didn't anybody try to help? She kept falling. She knew she would impact soon and it would be all over.

"GOOOOOD MORNING Glenhaven! This is your 6 a.m. wake up call. The sun is shining and you're gonna be late for work if you don't get those lazy bones outa bed and head for the shower. Here's a tune from the 70's that ought to get you moving...."

Emma's eyes opened wide with a start. She'd been dreaming again, this time seemed so much more real than the last several times. In fact, *over the last several months* she thought, *they seemed to be escalating in detail more and more.* The sheets beneath her were damp with perspiration. Why was she having these nightmares over and over. They began in her teenage years and as the years progressed they became more frequent and more vivid. Old houses, stores, streets she had never seen before and people with blank faces. It all seemed so real as though she had been there once. Yet, that was impossible since she had lived here in Glenhaven all of her life since early childhood when her parents moved here from New York. Her earliest memories were only of this small quaint town here in Connecticut. The places in her dreams however were definitely not of this town.

As Emma reached over to touch her husband's shoulder to wake him as she always did in the mornings, she reflected on the argument they had the night before at the dinner table. Bill had gotten so angry with her when she told him she would not be continuing with her therapist Dr. Fisher. The sessions weren't working at all and the dreams were just getting worse and more frequent she told him. Bill had never really understood about the dreams for all the years they were married. In the beginning he had been sympathetic but not really interested in exploring it any further. Emma dismissed it as his always being so busy with work. She tried not to bother him with it as the years went by.

Now his impatience seemed to only make matters worse. He would chide her about being driven "crazy" by all those teenagers at the high school where she taught. For some reason Emma hated it when he would say that. Being crazy was not at all what she felt with these horrible nightmares. Scared was a more appropriate feeling.
He would always tell her that he was only kidding when he would say that, but she sensed that he was actually thinking it might be true. In the last six months however he had conceded that maybe something might be causing their intensity and frequency, but he told her to do whatever she wanted to try and deal with it.

It bothered her immensely that her dreams seemed to simply take too much time from Bill's thought for him to be interested. Since he had gotten his promotion last year, he had been busier than ever and even though by his own admission to not being very popular at work for some reason, more and more of the staff seemed to be coming to him with problems at work. Bill's voracious appetite for success had cost him a few friends and associates over the years but he would simply say that it was their loss and move on. In fact, sometimes Emma felt like his ego just didn't have time for her little issues like these reoccurring nightmares.

Still, she thought as she gently shook his shoulder to wake him, *he wasn't so bad.*

"Come on Bill," she whispered. "Time to get up."

As he rolled over he looked up at her and immediately knew; she had had one of "those" dreams again. With a look of seeming frustration he said;

"You okay?" as he rolled out of the bed.

Emma simply nodded and took her robe from the chair, slipped it on and walked into the bathroom to prepare for work.

Bill came into the kitchen, as Emma was just putting the cat food down. She turned and spoke softly.

"Bill, this one was so real."

"Honey," he interrupted. "I'm really in a hurry this morning, can we talk about this tonight?"

Emma knew instinctively that meant he really didn't want to talk about it at all. She always held out hope that they would but she knew he'd find a reason not to. She nodded in resignation.

Bill picked up his briefcase and as he headed out the kitchen door to the garage he shouted back to her.

"Don't be too rough on those kids today."

As she watched him back out of the driveway she thought; *Too bad, he's really a good man.*

She turned and walked through the breezeway into the kitchen. She reached down and picked up the soiled rag she had dropped between the washer and dryer and now tossed it into the laundry basket. She stopped, turned and looked at the basket for a moment. *No* she thought, *probably shouldn't put that in with the clothes. The stains might come off on some of the other clothes and that would be bad.*

Emma left the house about 20 minutes later and as she

drove the short distance to Benjamin Waltham High School she thought about her lengthy career in education she had here in Glenhaven. It made her proud that last week she had been nominated for the third time in this many years for the state's highest award for teaching. Her mother was probably smiling down on her she thought, turning to whoever she was inhabiting that space with and saying, "That's my daughter."

Emma smiled as her thoughts were interrupted by the sound of a car horn. Emma looked around and pulling up on her right was Kathy Turner, president of their Soroptomist Club. She pulled even with Emma, lowered her window and shouted over.

"Hi. Congratulations. I heard about your nomination again. You're gonna win again for sure sweetie."

Emma smiled broadly and waved back.

"Thanks," she answered. "See you at the meeting on Tuesday."

The two women pulled away from the intersection, Kathy turning right and Emma continuing to school. This had always been a good town to her she thought. She had many friends and acquaintances and enjoyed being involved in as many social and civic organizations as she was. She hoped that it would never change.

Second period, U.S. History. After eight years Emma could almost do this in her sleep. As she was imparting to her youthful charges the importance of understanding the Depression Era, the door to her classroom opened. Standing in the doorway were the principle, Mr. Harris, her closest friend, and fellow teacher Susan, but more disturbingly, two uniformed Highway Patrolmen. Emma felt her heart skip a beat, maybe two. They just stood there for what seemed like minutes not saying a word. The classroom became eerily quite. Finally Susan stepped into the room and said softly

"Emma, come with us honey. Something has

happened."

At once Emma knew. As she exited the room she asked;

"Bill? Has something happened to Bill?"

Once outside the room the two patrolmen stepped forward.

"I'm sorry Ma'am," one of them said. "It appears that your husband has been in an accident."

"Is he okay?" Emma asked.

The officer lowered his head but before he could answer, Susan put her arm around Emma's shoulder and spoke.

"I'm sorry Emma. He's gone honey."

Emma felt her knees weaken and she felt as if she would faint and fall down right there. The two patrolmen were now on either side of her holding her up as they all proceeded down the hallway to Harris' office. Once there, Emma clutched at one of the officers sleeve and asked.

"Is he okay? Will I be able to see him?"

Susan took her hand and helped her sit down.

Turning to the patrolmen Susan said, "I'll take her home."

"Are you sure?" One of the officers asked. "We could call for paramedics,"

"No," Susan replied. "I'll call their family doctor and have him meet us at the house."

"We're going to need to talk with you further Ma'am, but not right now."

Emma felt as though everything was spinning around her as she held tightly on to her best friend's arm. Susan led her from the school out to the parking lot.

Leaving the school, traveling to the house, even meeting with the doctor all seemed to pass without her even realizing it. When she finally awoke and looked over at her alarm clock, she couldn't believe the time; 2:44 a.m.. She had slept all day and into the night. She figured the doctor must have given her a sedative when he was there. As she lay there in the quite solitude of the bedroom she had shared with Bill all these years, she found herself quietly humming. Not a tune she recognized, but just a repetitive simple tune. She felt relaxed at that moment and then suddenly, as if she had been "caught" doing something wrong she sat up abruptly.

The room was pitch black save the luminous digits on the table clock, yet she felt a presence there in the darkness. She slowly looked around the room. Her eyes, adjusting to the darkness seemed to make out a figure sitting in the old leather chair in the corner that Bill had always sat and read his business reports in. It was his thinking chair he would say. Many of his more unscrupulous ideas at getting ahead at the company had been concocted there. And now it felt to Emma as if Bill himself was sitting there watching her as she had slept. But no, it couldn't be. He could never have survived she thought.

Emma's palms felt sweaty as she reached for the bedside lamp. Would he haunt her forever in retribution she wondered. As she turned on the light, she now saw that in fact it was Susan asleep in the chair. What a faithful friend she was and had always been. Whenever Emma had needed someone to talk with, Susan was always available. And now, even though her own husband and children were at home, here she was staying with her through this terrible night.

Emma slowly got up from the bed and walked over to her vanity. She sat and stared into the mirror. Picking up her brush, she began combing her hair, slowly and deliberately at first as her thoughts began to drift. As she continued her gaze she felt almost as though she was drifting into a sleep as she methodically combed through her hair. She looked deeply into the mirror and seemed to see flames licking up behind her yet she couldn't break her trance. She heard muffled voices, screams coming from the flames. She began to feel pain on her head as though something was pulling at her hair violently.

As the flames seemed to consume the entire room around her now, she felt a strong tugging at her shoulder and a voice yelling her name.

"Emma, Emma, are you okay?"

Emma snapped out of the trance she was in as Susan was grabbing the brush from her hand. Emma reached up and touched her head and then looked at the brush in Susan's hand. Looking back at the mirror, she quietly said;

"It's just getting worse."

Susan knew exactly what her friend was talking about. Years earlier Emma had told her of the nightmares she had been having since early childhood. Emma also told her how her own parents seemed to scoff at the dreams calling them simply bad dreams and how her husband's lack of interest left her dealing with it alone. Susan was the one who had recommended Dr. Fisher, a therapist who had experience dealing with these sorts of things and yet he too was unable to bring about any rational explanation let alone any relief from them.

Emma got up and walked over to the bed where she sat up on the edge while Susan sat back down in the big leather chair in the corner. Emma's cat glided into the bedroom and jumped up into her lap. As the two women spent the remainder of the hours before dawn talking about Bill, and what comes next, Emma stroked the cat as it lay contentedly purring. Finally she drifted off to sleep. She knew it would only be for a few hours as so much needed to be attended to today.

The doorbell was ringing before seven. Anyone who had heard what happened were either calling or coming by sometime today. Students, faculty, friends, even neighbors. Emma thought how heartwarming it was to see this outpouring of sympathy from so many. Susan had promised to stay and help with the funeral arrangements and anything else Emma would need during these hours after her tragedy. Now, the doorbell awakened Emma and as she lay there she could hear muffled voices in the front room. She wondered who would have come by so early. She slowly rose up and putting on her robe, walked out into the living room. There she saw Susan sitting and talking with two men in suits. As she entered the room, the two men stood up. Susan spoke first.

"Emma, these men are from the Highway Patrol. They need to ask you some questions."

As the two stepped forward to shake Emma's hand, the shorter of the two men spoke first.

"Mrs. Holcomb, my name is Jim Burnside and my partner here is Bob Adams."

Emma felt uneasy with him right away. She couldn't place what it was exactly, just something about his demeanor or his appearance. His belly hanging over his belt, his tie loosened already, so early in the day and his suit, wrinkled as though he might have slept in it. But his voice bothered her most she thought. It was raspy, as though brought on by years of drinking or smoking. Come to think of it, she thought, he did smell a little of cigarette smoke. She hated it when people came in her home that smoked. They always left an odor in the air.

"Whenever there's an accident like this," he continued. "We have to ask some questions."

"We hate to have to come out so soon ma'am," the other officer added.

"That's alright," she said softly as she directed the two men to sit.

"Did your husband have his car worked on in the last few days or weeks?" Burnside asked.

"Not that I know of," Emma answered as she reached for the coffee Susan had brought in for them. "Oh yes, he did get the oil changed last week I believe it was. Why do you ask?"

Burnside responded quickly; "Just routine questions in situations like this."

- 91 -

There was that "situations like this" comment again Emma thought. Strange that he would repeat that.

"We understand your husband was pretty successful at his work wasn't he?" the other officer added.

Emma seemingly perturbed at the tone of that last remark answered; "Bill was good at what he did. What has that got to do with anything?"

Burnside chimed in; "Well, we spoke with his boss and some other folks down at his office yesterday and quite frankly ma'am, it seemed there might have been some animosities floating around there. In fact some of the people there didn't seem all that broken up that he wouldn't be returning."

"Bill was very competitive. Some of the others there were just jealous of his achievements," Emma said defensively.

"Maybe," he muttered.

"Did he ever talk about a co-worker named Stevens?" Jim asked.

"Only that he was surprised that he hadn't been fired by now," Emma answered.

Emma was quickly growing tired of these questions about her husband and his work.

"What is it you are looking for?" she asked pointedly. "I thought this was an accident."

"They're just some questions we have to ask in situations like this," Adams answered almost apologetically.

Growing increasingly angrier, Emma asked; "Just what kind of situation is this exactly?" directing her query to Burnside specifically.

As Susan watched quietly from her chair, she could almost feel the tension building between Emma and Jim Burnside. Emma was shifting uneasily on the couch as she waited for his reply. Burnside didn't respond but instead seemed to be trying to stare down Emma. The silence was finally broken moments later when the other officer said;

"We're really sorry for taking up your time like this and I

want you to know, we're very sorry for your loss. We hope everything will work out for you."

"You didn't answer my question," Emma said impatiently speaking directly to Burnside.

A moment passed and finally Burnside responded softly.

"An accident situation ma'am, an accident situation."

The two men got up and walked to the front door. Bob Adams turned and handed Emma his card.

"If you need anything ma'am, just call."

As they opened the door, Emma asked; "Was there anything left of the car?"

Adams turned and answered; "Not really ma'am, there was a fire and it didn't leave too much."

He looked at her knowing that the answer he gave was probably painful. "I'm sorry" he added.

He touched her arm and went through the open door after Burnside into the early morning sunlight.

As the two men walked to their car, squinting as he put his sunglasses on, Burnside turned his head towards his partner and said;

"Odd question don't ya think?"

Closing the door, Emma walked back into the living room. She sat down, poured herself another cup of coffee and mumbled a profanity under her breath clearly directed at the men who had just left. Susan had not said a word during the entire time they were there but rather, had been watching the interaction between Emma and the two officers. She had never seen Emma get quite so upset and out of character. Usually so articulate and gracious, this morning she seemed impatient and defensive. But surely the events of the previous day were taking their toll on her she thought. The rest of the day Susan stayed with Emma as she prepared for Bill's funeral and afterwards. That night, Susan went home.

The day of Bill's funeral arrived. Susan and her husband were right there to take Emma to the ceremony. Emma was surprised at how many people showed up. But she felt uneasy when she noticed that Jim Burnside was standing at his car the whole time. That didn't set well with her.

Afterwards, at her home many had gathered to offer their sympathies and to extend their help if needed. She couldn't wait for them all to leave. Susan once again handled everything allowing her to merely visit with her friends. After the last person had left, Susan sat at the front window quietly staring out as the afternoon wore on into early evening as if half expecting Bill to come up the driveway. Suddenly, a black and white Highway Patrol cruiser slowly drove by and Emma felt the hair on the back of her neck stiffen. She stood up and abruptly drew the curtains shut.

Several days passed and Emma found it nearly impossible to even get out of bed let alone make herself anything to eat. Susan came by on the third day. Using the key Emma had given her months earlier, Susan let herself in. She made her way into Emma's bedroom and finding Emma still laying in bed she walked over to the window and pulled the drapes back letting in the late morning sun.

"Today," she blurted out. "We're gonna get you out of this house even if it's just for a ride. You can't stay cooped up in this house. You're going to have to think about what you're going to do next," she added. "There are a lot of fertile minds over there at the school waiting for you."

"I don't know," Emma sighed as she drew the covers off her. "I don't know if I want to go back to school."

She got up and walked towards her bathroom thinking just how unsure of anything she was right now. She remembered how she and Bill had talked about traveling someday when they were through with their respective careers. Maybe now was the time.

Susan was successful at getting Emma out of the house that day. They drove through the Connecticut countryside stopping at a small café for lunch. They sat at an outside table enjoying the spring-like conditions. They talked for what seemed like hours about all sorts of things. Emma began telling Susan about some of her more recent dreams when suddenly without warning; Emma slammed her fist down on the table cursing the waitress for not having brought them a refill for their coffee by now. Susan sat back surprised, even shocked at this behavior Emma was demonstrating.

"Emma," Susan exclaimed. "What's the matter? I've never seen you like this."

Emma simply raised her eyebrow at Susan.

"Are you sure you really know me. I mean really know me?" she asked. "Sometimes I don't think I really even know myself."

As Emma gazed off into space, Susan signaled the waitress to bring more coffee.

"Sometimes, I feel so consumed by whatever it is that is causing these nightmares that I want to just give in to it," Emma said, sighing in resignation.

Susan just listened as Emma went on about these recurring nightly events that seemed to be consuming her friend. She wondered now if any of Emma's visits to Dr. Fisher had helped at all. This change in her friend's personality worried Susan but more so, it frightened her. The drive back was filled with uncomfortable silence. Later that night as Emma lay in bed trying to sleep but afraid to, she thought how empty her life seemed now. The house, the teaching, even this town seemed to hold nothing for her anymore. She ran her hand across the empty sheets beside her. She cried quietly.

Chapter Two

"Why are they bringing that heap here?" Sanchez asked as he and the dispatcher watched the flatbed tow truck backing the burned and twisted remains of Bill Holcomb's '85 Buick into the yard. "Haven't we got enough work to do?"

"Sometimes Burnside likes to see how we work under pressure," the dispatcher replied half laughing sarcastically.

"Put it over there in bay 6 next to that Mazda," Sanchez yelled out to the tow truck driver.

Turning to the dispatcher, Sanchez asked; "You wanna call Burnside and tell him it's here or you want me to?"

The dispatcher, reluctantly picking up the phone indicated he would. No one was thrilled when Burnside was in the building as he was always pushing hard for answers. Sometimes getting in the way of the technicians working there. And usually wanting answers sooner than they could be produced.

The Accident Reconstruction Lab was always a pretty busy place as any wreck that seemed in any way out of the ordinary was brought here for deeper scrutinizing. Six different counties utilized this one facility so there were always several investigations going on at once. If there were any questions about what happened during an accident that couldn't be answered at the scene, they could probably be answered right here. This had been home base for Jim Burnside for the past fourteen years. His fellow officers often called Jim's desk the Black Hole as he always had an array of papers, files, tools, dirty rags and such scattered across it. Today was no exception as he walked in and glancing over at the empty donut box he just grinned.

"You missed out Jim," Bob Adams said as he approached Jim's desk. "Where you been? They brought in the Holcomb Buick this morning."

"Checking on a few things," Jim answered. "Did you ever hear back from that lube place that did the oil change on that car?" Jim asked Adams as he walked towards the door to the garage.

"Yeah. They said everything was fine with the car when he left there," Bob yelled after him.

As Jim entered the garage and walked over to bay 6, one of the on-duty techs joined him.

"What are we looking for Jim?" He asked.

"Anything, anything at all. I don't like the way the scene looked. Something just doesn't look right. No skid marks. Nothing. The guy went right through the barrier like it wasn't even there."

"Alright, we'll get on it this afternoon," the tech offered as he dropped off to another bay where another vehicle demanded his attention.

Jim walked up to the wreckage of Holcomb's car. He stood there staring at it for a moment, then slowly walked around it as if looking for something to pop out at him.

"Come on, talk to me," Jim whispered.

It had been six weeks now since Emma had been back to the school. As she stood at the window of Mr. Harris's office staring blankly out the window, she began to speak.

"I've given this a lot of thought and I just can't come back. Everything has changed, it's so different for me now. I'm just not happy. I'm sorry I can't give you more notice, but the substitute you have in there for me is doing a great job and I'm sure she'll work out until you can find a permanent replacement."

"Well Emma," Harris answered. "The Connecticut school system is going to be losing one of it's finest teachers, but if this is what you have to do, then you have to follow your gut. You know I wish you only the best wherever you decide to go. I'm sure your mother would support you completely if she were here."

Emma nodded and turning from the window, she slowly walked out of the office, across the lobby and out into the sunlight. As she walked towards the teacher's parking lot for the last time, she thought about what Mr. Harris had said. Would her mother have supported her now? Even given the circumstances Emma couldn't imagine her mother graciously accepting her decision to leave teaching altogether. All she had ever wanted Emma to do was teach. She had drilled it into her head beginning at 5-years-old.

Nothing nobler than being a teacher, she would crow each evening as she graded her own student's papers at the kitchen table. When Emma went on to college to get her teaching credentials, her mother would go on and on to anyone who would listen. "You'll see," she would say. "My daughter's going to be a University professor one day." When Emma came back to Glenhaven to teach at the high school it almost seemed a disappointment to her mother yet she accepted it as though it were simply an interim assignment on her daughters way to greater achievements. And now, here she was. Walking away from it altogether. As she reached the car she turned around and glanced back at the school for the last time. A wry smile came across her face.

As she drove off she went over the checklist she had made for the journey she'd be taking in a few days so she wouldn't forget a thing. Everything was pretty much done she thought. It had all gone so smoothly. And Susan had assisted with so much. Deciding to close up the house had been quite the endeavor but with Susan's help, it all went well. At some future date Susan would help her get it on the market for sale from wherever she found herself. The insurance papers had been processed and the proceeds should follow Emma. She would provide them with an address once she got settled somewhere. Now Emma needed only to find a home for Snoball. She thought about simply turning it out that night but she and Bill had always agreed that the cat wouldn't last a night outside. Coyotes had regularly been seen in the hills behind the house and a cat would make an easy snack for them.

Now as she headed to Susan's house. She figured maybe she could meet up with best friend and grab some dinner one last time before she left. As she pulled up in front of the house she could see that Susan's car was not there so she sat back in her seat while the warm afternoon sun relaxed her and decided to wait.

They were laughing as they played by the side of the river. The little girl was running back and forth up and down the small embankment from the waters edge back up to the boy. She kept calling him to join her there by the water. She began taunting him, trying to get him to come down off the embankment. Finally he gave in and carefully came down to the waters edge. She splashed in the shallow part by the drop off that led to the deeper part of the river where the waters were moving much quicker. She laughed at his apparent apprehension to go near the water. She continued taunting him. Suddenly, she heard her name being called. There it was again. She turned to see where the calling was coming from. When she turned back towards the water she didn't see the boy anymore but heard her name being called again.

"Emma, Emma?"

Emma opened her eyes and saw Susan standing at her car window.

"Didn't you hear me call you?" Susan said. "You look

like you were off in a daze," she added as she leaned over and put her arms on the open car window. "Have you been here long?"

"No, only a few minutes I think. I must have dozed off," Emma answered. "I wanted to surprise you and see if we could grab some dinner on my last night here."

"Oh I can't tonight sweetie," Susan said "I'm meeting some buyers in twenty minutes to sign loan docs. I've already missed one meeting with them," referring to one of the times she was helping Emma recently.

Emma looked away and staring out the windshield replied in a somewhat disgusted tone;

"Fine. I guess I should have made an appointment since you're so busy."

She started her car up and was about to put it in drive when Susan reached in and turned the ignition off.

"Emma, what is wrong?" Susan asked cautiously.

After all these years being her best friend, Susan believed she knew Emma fairly well but the changes in her behavior lately truly troubled her.

"Is everything okay? Is there anything I can do?" she added.

Emma sat there for several moments just staring through the windshield. She finally turned to Susan and quietly said;

"I'm sorry, I guess my nerves are still a little frayed around the edges."

"Why don't I call you later this evening?" Susan offered.

Without even giving her friend a chance to step back, Emma turned the car on, put it in drive and slowly drove away without answering.

Susan stood in the street watching her friend disappear around the corner wondering what demons her best friend was struggling with.

As Emma continued driving home, she felt drained as she usually did upon waking from one of her nightmares. She remembered one of the things she had wanted to talk with

Susan about. She wanted to ask her about taking the cat.

It was just turning dark as Emma pulled into her driveway. As the headlights shone across the front of the house she noticed something on her front door. It appeared to be a note or a card. After she pulled into the garage, she walked around to the front door. Who could have been here while she was out? All of her business had been attended to and she wasn't expecting anyone. She pulled the business card off the front door and immediately recognized the official state logo on it.

Connecticut Highway Patrol
Accident Investigation Team
Inspector Jim Burnside

She turned the card over and scribbled in as poor a penmanship as she had ever seen was scrawled;

Please call me, J. Burnside

Emma unlocked the door and stepped inside. Tossing the card in the hallway trash, she went into her bedroom. Why were these people still asking questions she wondered? After all, it had been over a month now since the accident. What more could they possibly have to ask her about.

As she began getting ready to take a shower, she smiled and thought. How silly. He probably just wanted to tell her he was through with the report and was sending it along to the insurance company though; he could have just as easily called her with that information.

Coming out of the shower she felt completely relaxed and decided to lay back on the bed for a bit. As she sat down she gazed over at the leather chair in the corner of the room. She didn't even notice Snowball come into the room. It jumped up onto the bed next to Emma startling her. Placing her hand on her chest, Emma blurted out;

"You scared the crap out of me you little shit!" and she shoved the cat off the bed.

It immediately jumped back up and began walking in small circles next to Emma looking for that perfect place to lie down. Emma picked the cat up and drew it to her chest. As she sat stroking the cat's head and neck, she remembered how Bill had found it years before seemingly abandoned and brought it home. She had never really wanted a cat. It bothered her how Bill had always coddled it more than she thought necessary. She would comment that it needed to be more independent, but Bill was insistent that it be an indoor cat. As she lay back on her pillow she thought that she would really have to do something about this cat.

Emma woke in a pool of sweat. Her nightmare seemed once again to be so real. She lay there thinking that although she's never left Glenhaven, these places and people were so real to her. So much, like so many other times, she had dreamt this same dream. The sound of the phone ringing brought her back to the present. She figured it was probably Susan calling as she had said she would. Emma lay there letting it ring and ring deciding not to bother answering it. Finally the noise stopped and the room was once again quiet in the darkness of the hour. She fell back to sleep.

Chapter Three

D-Day. Departure day. Emma awoke early and as she lay there, she thought it would be difficult leaving friends and familiar surroundings. She had no relatives of her own after her mother died and Bill's were always a little standoffish, so leaving them wasn't really that hard. She got up and walked over to the sliding glass door that led out to the patio and the yard beyond. She slowly closed and locked it. As she showered and dressed and finished packing, she began getting excited about whatever the future was going to bring.

The house was locked up, the car was packed and she was heading out of her driveway as Susan pulled up in front of her.

Emma got out and met Susan at the end of the drive.

"I called and called last night but you didn't answer," she said with a genuine concern in her voice.

"Yeah, well, I was sleeping."

"Were you going to leave without saying goodbye?" Susan asked.

"I was gonna call you later when I stopped for breakfast," Emma replied.

She reached out and wrapping her arms around Susan, the two women hugged.

"You've been a good friend Susan and I love you for it. I will keep in touch," Emma whispered in her ear.

Emma turned and got back in to the minivan and waited for Susan to get back in her car and leave.

As Emma pulled out of her driveway and drove away,

she paid particular attention to all the beauty around her. The green rolling hillsides, the abundant trees, the flowers in her neighborhood. She got an uncomfortable feeling that she might never see any of this again and it made her sad. As she drove out onto the Interstate, she looked back in her rear view mirror but saw nothing.

She drove for hours only stopping briefly to grab a quick lunch and then back on the road. As the afternoon began to wane, she thought a quick stop for a coffee or soda might help with the drive. At this point she really didn't have a destination but somehow knew she had further to go.

Spotting the gas station ahead on the right, Emma decided she would fill up now instead of in the morning. As she pulled in she was glad to see that it included a mini mart where she would get her beverage.

After pumping her gas, Emma walked into the market to pay. As she entered she noticed a small group of people arguing at the counter. From what she could gather, apparently the young lady behind the counter had given their credit card to someone else who was now long gone. And of course now she couldn't accept the card she had. Emma poured herself a cup of coffee as she continued watching the commotion up front. It wasn't helping at all that the group was apparently Middle Eastern and was having some difficulty with the language. The girl behind the counter was having some difficulty understanding the broken English and what sounded like Farsi. She was obviously quite flustered by her mistake and they manner by which they were berating her. Emma walked over to the counter to pay for her gas and coffee but she couldn't even get close. More of the family had now poured out of the motor home they were all traveling in and had joined the fracas inside the store. Emma tried several times unsuccessfully to get the girl's attention behind the counter to try and pay and be on her way but the girl, so flustered, simply waved her arm at Emma and shouted; "I'll get to you when I can."

Emma continued waiting patiently for a few more

minutes and then once again attempted to get the clerks attention so that she could pay. All the time this entire family was shouting and waving their arms at this young girl behind the counter.

"Hold your horses!" the clerk dismissively addressed Emma again.

Okay, Emma thought, this isn't the way to behave regardless of the circumstances. Emma glanced at the family now nearly in a complete frenzy over this girl's mistake. They simply ignored her as well.

Emma raised one eyebrow, shook her head, turned and walked out of the store.

She heard the clerk yell after her over the ranting of the family at the counter.

"Hey, where are you going? Come back here!"

Emma smiled half laughing and raised her arm and directing her middle finger back at the store, got into her car and drove away. She smiled and quietly laughed for miles imagining the expression on that girl's face as she watched Emma drive away.

As daylight faded to darkness she knew she would have to find a motel to spend the night. Preferably one where there was a restaurant or diner nearby. An hour or so down the road, Emma spotted a vacancy sign and pulled in. Not exactly the Ritz Carlton but it would do for a nights sleep. She'd get back underway first thing in the morning.

After checking in and settling into her room, Emma called her friend Susan. She described the drive and related the story about the events at the gas station and market she had stopped at that afternoon. Susan was surprised at Emma's almost cavalier attitude about the whole incident. Not paying for something? Flipping the girl off as she left? These were dramatically uncharacteristic behaviors for someone Susan had always know to be so intensely honest and who's reputation some thought bordered on sainthood.

"You're not serious are you?" Susan asked. "That doesn't sound at all like you," she added.

"What do you mean? Of course I'm serious. The stupid little twit deserved it. I should have clipped those foreigners motor home as I left too," Emma responded sounding impatient with Susan's question.

She fell back on the bed laughing. Neither of them spoke for a few moments. Emma's mood changed as she sat up on the edge of the bed.

"Who the hell are you to judge me anyway?" Emma asked belligerently.

This took Susan aback seeing this other side of Emma she had never seen before.

"It's just that there are so many changes you seem to be going through lately sweetie," Susan said. "I just don't understand."

Emma waited a few moments.

"You don't have to understand. Nobody does!" she yelled as she slammed the room phone down on it's cradle almost knocking it off the nightstand.

Emma noticed the dog sitting to the left of her car. It's eyes; dark and glaring seemed to be set directly on her. She noticed the frothing at the corner of it's mouth, which usually was a sign that the dog might be rabid. It bared it's fangs and uttered a deep growl. Suddenly the dog got up on all fours and seemed to be moving towards Emma. Right then Emma noticed movement across the street at the entrance to the cemetery. It was a small girl, maybe 4 or 5-years-old coming out from the cemetery. At first she thought how odd that a child so young would be there but those thoughts were quickly replaced with fear as she noticed the dog on her left, turn and take an interest in the child across the street. As the child continued walking, the dog started moving across the street towards her, it's teeth bared and dripping saliva from it's mouth. The dog had to weigh somewhere around 80 to 90 pounds she thought. The young girl before her wouldn't stand a chance against this animal. Emma wanted to yell to the girl to run but when she opened her mouth, nothing happened. It was as though she was mute, unable to utter a sound. She froze, now even unable to move. She tried screaming but like before nothing came out. Frozen, Emma watched the inevitable horror unfold before her eyes. She knew what was about to happen, her senses told her she had to do something but it was as though she were being held down by some unseen force that prevented her from acting but instead wanted her to be witness to this horrible tragedy that was about to unfold.

Suddenly, as though slapped in the face, Emma focused on the child and the approaching animal. Laying on her horn, she pressed down hard on the gas pedal. She heard her tires squeal as she sped towards the girl hoping to position herself between the young child and the dog. The child, frightened by the screeching tires turned and ran across the front of Emma's car, directly into the path of the now charging dog. Emma screamed as she watched the snarling animal jump at the child and in one swift motion took the small child's head into it's massive jaws. There seemed to be blood everywhere, on the windshield, the ground, everywhere.

Emma turned her head on the pillow and looked over at the travel alarm she had placed there. 3:30 a.m.. She was shaking and felt the sweat on her neck and forehead. She stared at the ceiling for several moments as the shadows from the outside lights cast eerie patterns across it. One looked grotesquely like a dogs head. Emma reached over and turned on the small nightstand light. As she lifted her head she noticed a dark stain on her pillow. An icy chill ran through her body. There, smeared on the pillow was most clearly blood.

She quickly jumped out of the bed unsure if she would find more. Emma was overcome with fear and helplessness as she wondered if her nightmares were crossing over some unknown boundary and leaving remnants of themselves with her. But why she wondered. Weren't the dreams vivid enough? She must be going crazy she thought. She crept backwards from the bed into the bathroom. She reached in and turned on the light. As she turned and leaned on the sink trying to regain her composure, she looked up into the mirror. She felt as though she might laugh and cry at the same time.

How silly she now thought to have imagined something so bizarre could be happening when all she had done was to bite her lip in her sleep. Obviously the intensity of this latest nightmare had caused her to do it, and pretty badly at that, to have caused as much blood as she did. She should have realized immediately. Although it had been many years since she had done it, she remembered as a little girl that she would, from time to time, bite her lip in her sleep. She never understood why. She only remembered her mother getting quite angry with her for ruining so many pillowcases. To this day she still had the smallest scar on her lip as a result of all the times she had done it. When her mother mentioned it to her doctor during one of her regular pediatric visits, Emma remembered him asking her if she had been having any bad dreams. At the time, she didn't remember having any and told the doctor so. Emma's mother however seemed more disturbed about the incidents and sometimes Emma would overhear the adults talking on the porch late at night about childhood traumas and such. She never knew exactly what they were talking about, however when she got a little older she would ask her mother if she had ever been hurt as a child. Her mother would always reply; " Do you think your parents would ever let anything bad happen to you?" That was supposed to mean that nothing ever did and so she never really gave it any more thought over the years. It wasn't until many years later that so many questions would begin to surface.

As Emma left her room and drove across the Motel parking lot she stopped at the street entrance before pulling out. As she crept forward to see if any cars were coming, a man walking his dog approached. It was huge, probably a Great Dane and its head was practically even with the drivers window. As they came closer to the car, Emma froze. The man and his dog casually walked around the front of the car and proceeded down the sidewalk. Emma relaxed and half smiling now, she ran her tongue gently over the bruise on her lip, pulled out into traffic and drove away.

Several hours into her driving, Emma began thinking about her mother. Last nights dreams had triggered many thoughts today and as she drove on for miles, she started thinking about when she had first learned that she was adopted. It was a terrible day. Rainy and gloomy, Emma had gone up into the attic after school to look for any papers about her family. Her high school project that month had been to create a family tree and she was eager to find out as much about her ancestors as possible. Her mother was still at work and wouldn't be home for another two hours so she thought this would be a good time to start looking. As she poured through picture after picture she noticed that there really weren't any pictures of her before about 5 or 6 years of age.

Odd, she thought since her father was always taking pictures all the time. Maybe her parents had them put them away someplace else. She would ask her mom when she got home. It was a crushing blow when her mother sat her down later that afternoon and explained the truth to her. She had never suspected and might have never known if she hadn't been searching through the pictures and not found any of her younger ones. Unfortunately her mother couldn't give her all the answers she had regarding who she was and where she came from. She learned only that she had been adopted through a private agency that had years before, lost all of its records to a fire that destroyed the entire building and its contents. For whatever reason there also were no state records either and so no history could be gotten. After Emma went on to college, she made several attempts to try and find any remnants of her earlier life but was unsuccessful and so finally just gave up. After all, she thought, she had been adopted at such an early age, how much could there be to find anyway.

She remembered running up to her room and crying for hours.

Now as she entered yet another state on her journey she wondered if somewhere out there her biological mother ever wondered what had become of her.

Chapter Four

Emma pulled into the gas station way too fast. Her mind had been a million miles away when suddenly there was the exit. By the time she decided that she would stop here for gas, she narrowly missed clipping the sign board at the entrance to the station. Slipping into the gravel shoulder a little she kicked up quite a dust cloud before finally coming to a stop in front of the pump.

"You must have been really close to running out of gas," the attendant said laughingly as Emma rolled down her window.

"I'm sorry. I guess I wasn't paying much attention when I pulled in. Would you please fill it up?" Emma responded rather sheepishly.

"Sure thing. You want me to check under the hood too?" he asked as he pulled the hose from the pump.

"Thanks, that would be great," she called back as she stepped out of the car to stretch her legs. She had already been on the road since 6:30 this morning with only a short break for gas and lunch around 11. Now as she looked over at the clock above the shop door it read 5:37.

"You're a long way from home," he said noting her Connecticut plates. "On vacation or business?"

"Vacation I guess. Not sure yet," Emma offered.

"Goin' anyplace in particular?" the attendant continued.

This fifth degree was starting to annoy Emma as she responded;

"Actually, I'm not sure where I'm going. Guess I'll know

when I get there."

Emma looked around at the buildings nearby and noticed the restaurant across the road.

"Food any good over there?" She asked the attendant.

"Well, I've been eating over there nearly 12 years now and I'm still here so I guess it's okay," he jokingly replied.

Emma figured he would probably know, so since it seemed to be the only place near by, she'd might as well eat there. After paying for her gas, she drove across the road and parked in front of the restaurant.

Emma got out of her car and proceeded up the few steps to the front door of the restaurant. As she did she noticed a man seated inside at the window watching her as she approached. It made her a little uneasy. As she entered, she glanced over at the man. It appeared to her that he might even be homeless as his clothes were quite disheveled and it looked as though he might not have bathed in some time. He looked almost her age though the years clearly had not been good to him. But mostly it was the look in his eyes as he followed her movement across the restaurant that unnerved her the most. She took a booth on the far side of the room away from where the man sat. She felt more comfortable with as much distance between them as possible.

As Emma read over the menu, she noticed as she glanced over the rim of the menu that the man seemed to be straining to see where she had sat. She dropped her glance back to the menu so as not to give him any indication that she might be returning his stare. What did he want, she thought. Did she look familiar to him?

A waitress came to the table and asked if she wanted a coffee while she looked over the menu.

"Thank you," Emma replied.

As the waitress walked back to the counter to get the coffee, Emma noticed the man get up and walk over to the counter where the waitress was standing. He gestured as though to get the waitresses attention. Emma wondered what he was up to. As the waitress looked up, he spoke to her turning his body as though he didn't want Emma to see him speaking to her. Emma wondered what the heck was going on. Who was this guy? What was he asking her? It appeared like whatever he was saying, it was about her as the waitress looked over his shoulder at Emma and then listened to whatever else he was saying. He shuffled back to his seat and the waitress returned with her coffee. As she reached the table, Emma waited for a moment to see if she had brought some message from the man. When it appeared she was not going to say anything, Emma spoke.

"Excuse me but what did that man say to you over there at the counter?"

The waitress looked down at Emma curiously. Sure, look surprised as though you don't know what I'm talking about Emma thought.

"That man. At the counter just a minute ago?" Emma questioned.

The waitress, dropping her weight to one side and placing her hand on her hip replied.

"He wanted his toast well done honey, why?"

"Okay, now why don't you try telling me the truth?" Emma insisted.

"Lady, why don't you try minding your own business," the waitress responded sarcastically and in a tone several other patrons could not help to overhear.

"Now have you decided what you want to eat?"

She took Emma's order and grabbed the menu from Emma's hands. She turned and walked back over to the counter where she began whispering to a couple of the other waitresses and discreetly gesturing towards Emma's booth. Emma wanted to shout over at her to stop talking about her but decided not to. Instead, her attention returned to the man across the room. She could feel the anxiety building in her. She didn't want to make a scene but she wondered what would happen if she simply confronted this stranger. She sat there for 5 minutes debating whether to go over to him or to just forget about the whole thing. Her decision was made easier by the arrival of her food. The waitress practically threw the dish down on the table and left without saying a word.

Emma ate quietly wanting only to leave this place as quickly as possible. When she was almost through with her food, she noticed the man get up and start walking towards her. She felt tightness in her throat. She thought she might choke on her food as she slipped further into the booth to distance herself from the aisle. Just as he was about five feet from her table she noticed him slow and hesitate for a moment. Her heart beating so strongly now, she imagined he must be able to hear it. Why was he tormenting her so? What could he possibly want from her? Emma was about to call out to him to stay away when he picked up his pace and strode past her table and into the men's room down the hallway behind her. She breathed a deep sigh of relief. She thought she might leave now while he was in the restroom or if she should just forget this silliness and ignore him altogether. After all, he hadn't said anything to her. Maybe he really wasn't looking at her. Emma sat there for a few more moments but then she heard the eerily creaking sound of the restroom door as it opened and the sound of his footsteps across the linoleum floor as he once again approached her table from behind her. Suddenly his footsteps stopped right behind her. She panicked and turning in her booth she cried out.

"What the hell do you want with me. Leave me alone!"

The stranger looked down at her and with one eyebrow lifted he sneered at her.

"Well, what do you want?" she yelled.

By now everyone in the restaurant was looking to see what the commotion was. The stranger stood there staring at Emma for what seemed an eternity then leaning over and putting his face directly in front of hers he whispered.

"You're from Hell lady. Go back there," He stood up and walked out of the restaurant.

The stench of his breath and un-bathed body caused Emma to reel back in her booth. She never took her eyes off him as he left the restaurant and walked out to the highway. It was dark now and she couldn't see him anymore.

It took her a full five minutes to compose herself. Most of the other patrons had returned their attention to their own tables. As the waitress threw the check down on Emma's table she said;

"You're crazy lady. Why don't you just get out of here."

Emma gave her a cold stare and immediately rose from her seat almost pushing the waitress to one side. She left the check and money on the counter as she hastily left the restaurant. Once outside she almost ran the few feet to her car. She fumbled with her keys trying to get into her car as fast as she could. Once inside, she started the engine and reached back to put on her seatbelt. As she was doing this a shadow of a figure appeared over her shoulder at the window. Emma screamed as she jammed the gearshift into drive and sped away. She left the figure standing amidst the dirt and gravel she had kicked up with her tires as she sped away.

There, dusting himself off with his hat stood the gas station attendant who had so graciously served Emma earlier. Mystified by her behavior he could only mutter.

"Guess she didn't want her change."

The sun was dropping rapidly and the shadows of dusk were all around her as Emma sped along the deserted highway. She had driven non-stop all afternoon and was getting tired. As she approached a curve in the road ahead, she noticed a figure by the side of the road. She recognized it as the man from the diner earlier that day. His arm outstretched, his finger pointing towards her. Emma screamed and slammed hard on her brakes. She cringed at the sound of the tires screeching on the pavement as she brought her minivan to a stop not twenty-five feet from him. Was he waiting for her? She thought. How did he get so far ahead of her? Emma quickly glanced ahead and through the rear view mirror, behind her. The highway was deserted as far as she could see. For a split second she contemplated throwing the van in reverse and turning around in the direction she had come. But to turn around would take too long she thought. He could be upon her in seconds. Emma stared at the figure before her. He in turn made no move but simply stared back at her dropping his arm very slowly as though he were waiting for Emma's next move. What could this stranger possibly want with her, she wondered. Didn't he understand her back at the diner when she told him to leave her alone? She would have to make him understand. Emma slammed her foot down on the accelerator and aiming her vehicle directly at him, she sped forward. She covered the distance between them in mere seconds. As her tires slipped on the gravel from the shoulder, the stranger leapt out of the way and down the embankment. Emma's heart pounded as she sped away glancing only once in her rear view mirror to see if she had hit him. She saw, now standing in the dust she had created, the figure of the man climbing back up onto the roadway and extending his middle finger at her. She didn't look back after that.

Emma tried blinking back the weariness that was descending even more rapidly upon her now as she continued driving through the night. She wanted to put as much distance between her and that stranger as she could and figured she would drive until it was daylight. But the hours of long driving as well as the emotional strain of all that had transpired in the previous day were becoming too much to fight. 2:20 in the morning the dashboard clock shone in the darkness. She could count on one hand the number of cars she had passed since the sun went down. She would have to stop soon she thought, but where?

Emma reached around on the seat next to her for the map she had tossed there the day before. She raised it up to read but it was too dark to make anything out on it. Not really wanting to, but realizing she needed to stop in order to see the map, Emma pulled over onto the side of the road. She looked around her at the complete blackness outside. It was eerily silent and there were no lights anywhere. The highway seemed so desolate as though no one ever traveled it, yet it appeared to be a main Interstate according to her interpretation of the map. She pulled the map light away from the dash and held it over the papers in her hand. According to the direction she had been traveling and the length of time she had been driving she should have passed at least one or two of the small towns shown on the map. She didn't remember seeing even one. Could she have been so obsessed with driving that she didn't even notice one of the turnoffs, she wondered. Whatever the case, she only knew that now she really needed to find a town where she could rest. Turning the map under the light she tried to get her bearings. She noticed that a small town appeared to be only a few miles ahead and off to the right, a relatively short distance from the highway.

She smiled a bit at the name of it. Jolene. She had always thought that name would have been a nice name for a girl had she been able to have children. Bill had always thought differently. Laying the map down next to her, Emma pulled back up onto the highway and proceeded to drive on. Only a few miles ahead, she saw the sign for Jolene, 8 miles to the right. Emma pulled off the highway onto the narrow dirt road. She hoped that they would at least have a decent motel where she could sleep.

As Emma turned the minivan onto what appeared to be the main street she thought, this was indeed a small town. There was but one stoplight several blocks ahead and no other lights were visible. Everyone seemed to be asleep save a lone dog that sauntered across the road in front of her. As she approached the end of the main street, a small neon light with an obvious short in it stuttered out the word VACANCY.

The building looked as though it might have been one

of the original structures, as it was old and fairly broken down. Nevertheless, Emma needed sleep and this was as good a place as any. As she approached the building she could make out the glow of a TV in the front window and a figure sitting inside. Good fortune, she thought that someone would be awake in the middle of the night to check her in.

"Mornin'," the old man mumbled without looking up as Emma entered the lobby.

"S'pose you'll be need'n a room?" he asked.

He rose and slowly turned a registration card around on the counter and slid a pencil towards her.

"Twenty four dollars for the night less o'course you're planning on stayin' longer," he said as he turned and reached for a key from the row of pigeon holes behind him.

"I'll only be staying the one night, thank you," Emma replied wearily as she filled out the registration card.

She reached into her purse and handed the old man two twenty-dollar bills.

"Got no change this late. Have to wait for the morning man to get your change less o'course you'll be payin' for more nights," he said somewhat angrily.

Emma was too tired to worry about her change right now and replied;

"That's fine," as she turned and walked towards the exit.

The old man stared after her and just as she was turning the knob on the door he added;

"Sure you won't be stayin longer?"

Odd, she thought, that he would be insistent about that after she had already stated that she was only interested in the one night.

"No, like I said, just the one night. Why do you ask?" Emma asked.

As the old man lowered his head and looked out at Emma over the rim of his wire glasses, he didn't say a thing. Then nodding as though disbelieving the answer she had given him, he turned back towards the TV, sat down and closed his eyes. Emma turned and walked out into the night. As she walked the short distance to her car she thought how odd this old man was to think that she would be staying any longer than she had said.

Emma pulled her overnight bag and one small suitcase out of the minivan and set them down in front of her room. She slid the key into the lock and shoved open the door. As she turned to pick up her bags, she glanced back at the office. There in the window was the old man staring at her. He reached up and pulled the string on the VACANCY sign. It went off and the area became dark.

Emma felt a chill slip through her body as she turned, went into the room and hastily locked the door.

Chapter Five

The little pink slip taped to his phone was the third one Jim Burnside had seen there over the past two days.

"*Please call Ted Rutherford, Guild Insurance*" was the message scrawled across it.

Why didn't the receptionist ever check the little boxes. Instead she always just scribbled across the sheet and it usually wasn't all that legible.

Jim didn't want to call this guy back unless he had something definitive he could tell him. So what if the Holcomb widow was anxious for the life insurance. They'd all just have to wait until he was through with his investigation, and he wasn't done yet. Not by a long shot.

As Jim entered Howard's office he already knew he was about to get his ass chewed. Howard Steinam was the head of the Connecticut Highway Patrol Accident Reporting Office and he oversaw all the lead investigators. He was always riding Jim for taking so long to close a case. He and Jim would continually go round and round but in the end, Howard would have to grudgingly admit that Jim was, if nothing else, thorough in his investigations.

"Jim," Howard barked "Why the hell don't you have this Holcomb thing wrapped up?"

Jim's partner, Bob, was already seated as Jim slid into the other leather chair across from Howard's desk.

"We're still interviewing a few of the husband's co-workers and neighbors. There's just something off with this one," Jim responded.

"Bob here says you haven't gotten everything back yet on the car?" Howard asked.

"We're going over to the shop this morning," Jim answered.

"Well let's try and get a fire lit under this okay? I've got cases backing up all over the place," Howard said irascibly. "Now get out of here and do your job."

"Will do chief," Jim answered as he and Bob got up and walked out of the office.

Once outside Bob asked;

"What's eating him?"

"Budget cuts," Jim answered.

"Why don't we go on over to the lab and see if we can hustle this thing along some," Bob said as the two men reached the elevator to the parking garage. As the doors closed behind them Jim replied;

"Might as well. Maybe we'll get lucky."

The Lab was very much like a large hanger. Metal building, large open doors; skylights on top and every type of test that could be performed on every possible part of a vehicle were done here.

Jim flashed his identification badge to the young lady seated at the front counter. She reached under her desk and buzzed them in through the main door. Jim led the way down the long corridor as they made their way left and right through the maze of cubicles. Each cubicle was an office for the inspectors that worked there. Almost reaching a dead end in one of the corridors, Jim poked his head into one of the offices. Not finding who he was looking for, he turned and looked into the office across the way.

"Where's Fred?" he asked the woman working at her computer terminal. Without looking up she replied;

"Out in the shop."

Jim turned and Bob followed as they made their way to the

exit out to the shop. Once out there, they stopped, and reaching to look over the many vehicles and equipment, they searched for where Fred might be working.

"Help you find someone?" a worker asked as he approached them.

"Looking for Fred," Bob answered.

The worker turned and pointing across the shop said;

"I think he's over there in bay 12."

"Thanks," Bob said as the two men made their way to where the worker had directed them.

As they approached the bay, Jim saw Fred with his head buried under the hood of a pretty severely damaged pick up truck. He knocked on the roof as he walked around to what was left of the front end of the truck.

"Fred," Jim shouted over the sounds of the machinery "Why haven't you called me back?"

Fred jumped back from under the crumpled hood and with a look of surprise on his face responded;

"I only got my results back yesterday. I was gonna call you this afternoon."

"So?" Jim queried.

"Well, mostly you've got nothing. Some fingerprints, mostly smudged but that bag you brought me? Well, this is probably what you wanted," Fred answered as he reached for and lifted up a plastic bag with a metal washer inside for Jim to see.

He pulled a pen from his pocket and pointed to a small dried smear on it. He looked over at Bob and then at Jim as he spoke.

"Brake fluid. Not too old either."

Jim Burnside smiled.

"Go ahead and send it over, and thanks," he said as he turned and walked away.

"Where'd you get that Jim?" Bob asked as they continued walking towards the exit.

"Remember that day after Holcomb's funeral when his missus had those people back at her house? Well I was

- 122 -

standing in the driveway and noticed her garage door was open and there was a small pool of something right about where the car should be. That washer was sitting right in the middle of that small pool of fluid. It was just laying right there in plain sight on the floor by the entrance so…"

"You just picked it up?" Bob asked surprised.

Jim smiled as they walked out into the morning daylight.

"Yeah, but that could have been a simple leak. It was an older car after all," Bob said.

"Yeah," Jim answered, "But then there was that Chilton's manual on the bench."

Pursuing the leads Jim had seen during this investigation had taken him in several different directions and had stretched the normal time frame for resolving an incident like this out much further than he or his superiors had hoped. First there was the possibility that this was indeed simply an accident. Then the tone Jim detected from some of the associates at Holcomb's work certainly caused him to look at the possibility of a jealous co-worker and now the discovery of brake fluid on the floor of the garage at his home opened up even more possibilities. Clearly Ted Rutherford at Guild Insurance and Howard Steinam were just going to have to show more patience while Jim dug deeper.

"Thank you for coming by," Jim said as he motioned for Emma's best friend Susan to take a seat in the chair across from his desk.

"Not a problem," she replied as she sat down "I had to come into town today anyway. How can I help?"

"Well, I'm trying to wind this thing up and wondered if maybe you could tell me about the Holcomb's," Jim explained as he leaned back in his leather chair. "For instance, how well did you know Emma and her husband? Did they get along well?"

"I've known Emma for 15 years but to tell you the truth, I really didn't know Bill all that well. He kept mostly to himself. Seemed like he was always working, so he wasn't around all that much. Emma and I would do a lot of stuff together, especially on the weekends. She and I became close friends very quickly and we were always there for each other."

Jim sat quietly for a moment before he continued with his questions.

"I understand Emma was seeing a shrink. Can you tell me what that was all about?"

"Dr. Fisher, sure. I recommended him to her quite some time ago because she was having these reoccurring nightmares and she seemed to think that Bill had become disinterested in hearing about them over and over. Apparently she had been having these dreams going all the way back to her childhood. She really needed to talk to someone other than me and I thought Dr. Fisher would be the perfect person for that. Have you spoken with him?"

"Not yet," Jim replied. "What would you say her state of mind was in the past few months?"

"I guess you could say she was just frustrated at not being able to understand why she was having these nightmares, but also frustrated that her husband just wasn't listening anymore. I'm sure Dr. Fisher could give you more information about that."

"So I'm guessing with her husband gone as much as he was, that Emma was pretty handy around the house with fixing things and such? Good at using tools maybe?"

"Well, she liked gardening but I don't know about fixing things," Susan answered. "Why do you ask?"

"Oh, no reason," Jim replied. "Well, like I said before, thanks for coming by today. I guess that's about all I had to ask you about."

Susan rose from her seat as Jim got up and walked to the door. As Susan was about to leave he asked;

"By the way, have you heard from Mrs. Holcomb since she left on her vacation?"

"It's been a few days now, but she'll probably call me this weekend."

"Do you know where she's going?" Jim asked.

"I'm not really sure. She hasn't told me yet. She just wanted to get away and try to clear her head of all this. Losing her husband has to have taken a real toll on her," Susan offered as she stopped and turned to Jim. "Those last few days before she left she really was on edge."

Jim pursed his lips and nodded as if understanding how she must have felt.

"Well, thanks again," Jim closed his office door after Susan exited and walked back over to his desk.

He picked up his notes and flipping through the pages stopped at one entry:

Dr. Eugene Fisher. Clinical Psychiatry.

He would call him now to set a time to meet. A knock at his office door and his partner, already walking in, stopped Jim from making the call at that moment.

"So, did her friend have anything more to add?" Bob asked.

"Not much," Jim answered. "But I think we're gonna want to speak with her shrink."

Jim picked up the phone and dialed Dr. Fischer's number.

Chapter Six

What a way to start the day she thought as she looked down at the flat tire on the minivan. Must have picked up a nail or something along the road coming into town last night, Emma thought. As she stood there she noticed a young man approaching from the direction of the office.

"Excuse me, could you help me here?" she called out raising her arm just enough to get his attention.

"Sure, what can I do for you?" he said enthusiastically.

"Well, I seem to have gotten a flat tire and I'm really not into changing it," Emma said almost apologetically.

"No problem," the young man answered as he leaned down on one knee to take a closer inspection of the flat.

"Hmmm," he mused as he scratched his head and looked up at Emma.

"What?" Emma asked.

"Looks like your tire's been slashed more than just an ordinary flat," he said.

"Slashed!" Emma exclaimed. "Who would do such a thing?"

"I don't know," he answered as he rose up. "No problem though, I'll call George up at the station and he'll send someone right over to fix it. You wait here, I'll be right back."

With that the young man turned and ran back over to the office and went inside. Emma figured that the old man last night was probably this boys grandfather. In a small town like this it was probably easy to have generations working at the same business. A few minutes passed and the young man returned. As he approached Emma he said;

"It's gonna take a few minutes longer 'cause George can't send somebody right away. Is that okay?"

Emma nodded. She figured she wasn't going anywhere anyway, so a few more minutes wasn't going to hurt

"By the way," the young man said as he reached towards Emma. "Here's your change from last night. We never keep any money in the till after ten o'clock. Hope you didn't mind."

Emma smiled and nodded her approval.

"If you want to, you could go have breakfast and your car should be done by the time you get back," the boy offered.

"Is there a place nearby here?" Emma asked.

"Sam's is on the next block and around the corner. You can't miss it," he told her as he pointed in the direction of the diner.

Emma briefly thought about the events of yesterday but then countered those thoughts with the rationalization that she couldn't run away from something she didn't even understand. She might as well get back into her vacation mode and this was as good a place as any.

"Thanks, I think I'll do that. Just up the block you say?" Emma asked as she turned and started walking towards the exit out to the street.

"Two blocks and turn right," the young man answered.

As Emma came out from under the overhang at the entrance to the motel, she stopped momentarily in the bright morning sun. She looked up and down the street of the small town noticing the different buildings and storefronts. Odd, she thought. How familiar theses surroundings seemed to her. Silly, she thought. She'd never been here before. As she turned to start walking towards the restaurant, she suddenly felt a wave of nausea come over her. She felt light headed as one might feel before they faint. Emma reached over to hold on to the side of the building. She took a step to let herself lean on the brick surface for support. She stood there for a moment hoping she wouldn't fall. She glanced back through the underpass of the entrance to the motel. There in the window of the office stood the old man from last night. Simply standing there, he made no motion to assist her and held an almost contentious look on his face.

As suddenly as this feeling had come upon her it washed away leaving her standing against the building. Emma wondered if perhaps she just hadn't gotten enough sleep. As she continued to stand there for a few more moments focusing on her surroundings, she noticed a few elderly people standing across the street. Surely they had seen her stagger to the wall and yet they made no move to assist her. Instead it appeared to Emma as though they were in fear of her for some reason. They scurried away whispering and gesturing back towards her until they were out of sight.

Crazy old biddies, she thought. Just her luck she'd stumble into a town where the old folks would think every stranger was trouble.

As she entered the diner she felt uneasiness come over her again. It felt as though several eyes were upon her, as the diner seemed to fall silent upon her arrival. At least a few of the other patrons, mostly the older ones were looking at Emma, a stranger to them who had entered their routine this morning. Silly, she thought as she made her way to a corner booth. She didn't know these people and they didn't know her. She had never been here before and yet something about this place gave her the willies.

The only waitress in the place looked as though she might have worked there her entire life. She was at least sixty if she was a day. Her hair was all white and she looked as if she drank most of life. Her eyes were all puffy and her nose was reddish and wrinkled as if alcohol were a standard part of her diet. Emma looked down at her menu and ignored anyone else. She was fairly absorbed in the choices on the menu that she didn't even hear the waitress when she asked what she wanted. Suddenly she noticed the tapping of her pencil on the table. Emma looked up.

The waitress suddenly turned absolutely white as if

she had seen a ghost. She half covered her mouth and stumbled backwards almost falling. Her order pad and pencil fell from her hands. Pointing at Emma, she screamed uncontrollably. Her eyes rolled back in their sockets as though she might faint. She grasped at the nearest table to balance herself and then, still screaming she turned and ran out the front door of the diner and down the street never looking back.

As Emma looked on, horrified, several people that were seated nearby quickly got up and moved away, all the time watching Emma suspiciously.

The cook came running out from behind the counter where he had been standing and running across the diner towards Emma's booth he yelled;

"What's going on here? What did you do to her?"

"I didn't do anything," Emma answered defensively. "I didn't say a word!"

"Well you must have said something or she wouldn't have gone off like that. She's been here over 40 years and she's never acted like that before," the cook yelled as he sat down across from Emma. "Honestly lady, you must have done something to spook her like that."

"I'm telling you, I didn't do a thing. Ask these people here," she said as she gestured to the few people who were now returning to their tables. "I didn't do anything did I?"

"I didn't hear her say anything Sam," said one man as he sat back down directly behind Emma.

Sam looked back at Emma and spoke.

"Well, I think we'd better go over to Flo's place and see what this is all about. You'd better come with me."

"Why me, I don't know what's wrong with your waitress. Why don't you just go over there?" Emma answered nervously.

"Look lady, you apparently caused this so you're coming with me or would you rather I call the Sheriff?"

Emma was visibly shaken by what had just taken place, but she too was curious as to why this woman had reacted the way she did.

"Alright, let's go," she said as she slipped out of the booth and followed Sam to the exit.

As the two of them left the diner, the cook introduced himself. "My name's Sam Woods. I bought this place back in '76 and Flo came with it. None of the other gals seem to last very long but Flo comes in, rain or shine every day of the week, every week of the year. Her mother worked in the joint before her. That'll give you some idea of how long this place has been around. She and her family have lived down here at the end of this road as long as anyone can remember. Her folks use to own it once upon a time. Now it's just a boarding house but Flo is a permanent resident there," Sam continued. "Flo never bothers anybody. Keeps mostly to herself and the only friends she has are a few of the older folks living here. I swear I've never seen her act anywhere like this as long as I've known her."

Emma was silent as they crossed the corner towards what appeared to be the oldest house in town. At one time it was probably a large family home. It appeared to date back to the late 1800's or early 1900's. Now it was sectioned up into a boarding house and left to fall into a sad state of disrepair. As they approached the front of the house, Emma noticed a couple of very old women sitting on the porch of the house next door. As she looked over at them they immediately got up and hurried inside. Sam didn't see it but it bothered Emma as their behavior was reminiscent of what had happened earlier outside the motel.

As they entered the front door, Emma looked up at the long staircase to the landing that loomed above her. A cold chill swept over her body and again an incredible wave of nausea seemed to take control of her body. She grabbed at the door handle and fell back against the wall.

"Are you alright?" Sam asked as he turned to steady her.

Emma stood there silent for a moment and slowly took in her surroundings. Why did she suddenly feel so sick and why did she feel a cold shiver streak through her body. Why

- 130 -

too did she sense that this was not all new to her but that there were uncomfortable feelings of familiarity to all of this? Sam tugged at her coat and said;

"Come on, let's go up and see if we can find out what's bothering Flo."

Sam placed his hand under Emma's elbow and began to guide her towards the staircase. Emma could barely walk now as this sense of utter fear swept over her entire being.

"I can't go on," she whispered. "You go ahead."

"Uh, uh, lady, you caused this, you're coming with," Sam said as he turned to help Emma up the stairs but she froze at the first step.

She clutched at the large knob at the base of the banister. Suddenly an old woman came running to the top of the staircase yelling.

"Help! Come quickly somebody! She's dead! She'd killed herself. Hurry please!"

Sam turned quickly and letting go of Emma's arm and taking two steps at a time he raced up the stairs to where the old woman was standing and pointing down the hall.

Emma sank slowly down to sit on the first step. She knew she couldn't go up there. She already knew what had happened. A door across from where she sat opened and an old man stuck his head out, looked around and asked.

"What's all the commotion?"

Emma, now feeling a sense of calmness come over her looked up slowly and in a soft voice answered;

"The old bag killed herself."

Emma got up and walked out of the house now feeling completely composed once again.

Upstairs, Sam couldn't believe what he was seeing. Flo had hastily strung an old lamp cord up over the rafter above the kitchen table. She was hanging limp where she had kicked a chair away from under her. Obviously it hadn't taken long for her aged body to succumb to the trauma of having the cord so tightly around her neck. It had clearly snapped her neck as her head fell to one side.

Sam stood in the doorway for several long moments just nodding his head in disbelief and mumbling.

"Why? Why?"

The old women who had discovered her leaned against the doorframe sobbing quietly.

Sam finally turned and went downstairs and out of the house. Sheriff Wentworth had just pulled up when Sam had begun walking over toward Emma who was sitting on the grass in front of the house.

"Lady, I don't know what's going on here but I'm certain the Sheriff is going to have a lot of questions for you," Sam said as he gestured to the Sheriff to come over to them.

Emma looked over as the Sheriff stepped out of his truck. He seemed to her a giant of a man. He affected an intimidating silhouette with the morning sun behind him. The only distinguishable feature she could make out were his boots as he strode towards where she was sitting. The intricacy of the tooling on the leather was somehow familiar to her but from where she couldn't place right now in the midst of this incredible situation.

"What's going on here Sam? I got a call that someone's gone and hung themselves?" the Sheriff asked.

"It's true Charlie. This lady here said something to Flo over at the diner and she ran screaming out of my place, came home here and strung herself up," Sam answered.

Emma now jumped up and placing her face within inches of Sam's she yelled;

"I told you I didn't say a word to her. I didn't get a chance to."

Now directing her comments to both Sam and the Sheriff she continued;

"She just came over to my table, I looked up and she freaked out. I didn't say a word to her."

The Sheriff stepping between Emma and Sam asked;

"Well, Sam?"

"Well the people sitting next to her said they didn't hear her say anything," Sam answered. "But I don't know why Flo would just up and do this if she didn't do anything."

The Sheriff turned and gave Emma a 'once over' before he spoke.

"Ma'am, maybe you could tell me who you are and what you're doing here?"

Emma looked straight at the Sheriff and answered;

"Officer, I swear to you, I have no idea what happened here. My name is Emma Holcomb. I'm a schoolteacher from Connecticut. I'm traveling on vacation and I stopped here in this town last night to get some much-needed sleep after driving all day. I wake up this morning and find my tire has been slashed. I come down to his place for breakfast while they're fixing it and this all happens. I don't know if she mistook me for someone else or what, but she took one look at me and went running out of his restaurant. I came over here with him to see if I could find out why she ran away. That's all I can tell you cause that's all there is."

Turning to Sam the Sheriff asked;

"Sam?"

Sam shrugged his shoulders and made an expression as though to confirm that the story rang true.

"Ms Holcomb, you are planning on being in town for a little while aren't you?" the Sheriff said in a tone that was more a statement than a question.

"I'll stay as long as you need me too," Emma answered.

She too wanted to get some answers to a few nagging questions she had herself.

By now a crowd had gathered on the street in front of the old house. News travels fast in a small town like this. Two more Sheriff cars pulled up. As the other officers were putting up yellow tape around the front of the property, most of the people were straining to try and see what had happened. Emma noticed several much older towns people near the back of the crowds seemingly watching her. They whispered among themselves. She wondered what they might be saying as she had this eerie feeling that they were talking about her. She supposed that they must think that she was involved in some way. Made sense after all, the Sheriff was talking with her. It was something more though. Something that made Emma feel angry. She must have conveyed those thoughts in her appearance as she stared back at them for they suddenly turned and hastily walked to the house next door. Once upon the porch, the other two women Emma had seen earlier ushered them into the house. They seemed frightened. Not so much by what had happened but more so by seeing Emma. She remembered the older folks she had seen across from the motel that morning. They too seemed frightened, as they also had quickly run away. What was it about herself Emma thought that made these people react the way that they had. She needed to get some answers. She was about to walk right over to the house next door when a voice spoke from over her shoulder.

"Somehow this really doesn't surprise me," the voice said.

Emma turned and there stood a man around 50 or so, she thought, scratching his forehead and addressing her.

"Everybody knew she was crazy as a loon," he continued. "Used to go around here predicting her own death. Kind of morbid."

"Excuse me?" Emma said. "Did you know her?"

The old man gazing off towards the old house answered.

"Only as much as anyone who hasn't lived here as long as she has does. She was always kind of a recluse ya know. Stayed pretty much to herself. Went to work, came home. That's about it," he went on. "Oh, I'm sorry, here I am going on and I haven't rightly introduced myself. I'm Pete Dougherty. I run the local paper here, such as it is," the man said extending his hand out.

Emma took it and shook his hand. As she did a foreboding sense of ill swept over her. It wasn't the man before her so much as it was a sense that meeting him would bring all of her horrifying dreams screaming back to her. She pulled her hand from his quickly and drew it up to her chest as though stung by a shot of electricity. She turned and glanced at the porch next door. The curtain in the front window dropped as the old man standing before her continued talking.

"Yep, wife and I moved up here in '66 and bought the paper for something to do. She passed on a few years back, but I still keep those old presses running every week. This'll keep them talking for a while."

Emma turned back toward the man who called himself Pete and asked;

"You say you knew her somewhat?"

"Well, like I said," he answered "Not too much. Just know that she was one of the oldest residents here. Born here. Lived here all her life. Worked over at Sam's since she was a kid according to some of the older folks around here. She had a sad life though. Parents both died when she was around fourteen and then a few years later her sister, poor girl, got attacked by that dog. Ripped the poor girls head clean off."

Emma stood speechless, almost in shock at what she was hearing.

"Do you know how the parents died?" Emma asked.

Pete raised an eyebrow as though he thought that a peculiar question, but then replied.

"Don't know for sure, but I've got lots of old newspapers that probably have something about it in them."

"May I see them?" Emma asked.

"Well sure you can, but why would you want to if you don't mind me asking," the old man said.

"Just curious," Emma answered

"Well, come on over after one and I'll show you all the papers that are up in the attic. You'll probably find something there."

Emma knew she had to go and see those papers. Something seemed to compel her to do so yet, something also left her with a sense that there were answers there that she might not really want to know. She turned and walked back to the motel.

All the way back to the hotel, Emma felt a chill permeate through her entire body, even though the day was warm and sunny. Why, she wondered, did she feel so uneasy since arriving in this town? Why too were so many unusual things happening? And adding to her confusion was the eerie feeling that there were so many things about this town that seemed vaguely familiar when she knew she had never been here before. Could this place have been in or played some sort of role in her nightmares?

As she turned the corner and approached the entrance to the motel, Emma noticed the shadow of a man standing in the driveway just under the overhand she had passed through this morning. Suddenly, once again, the fear from yesterday swept over her almost choking the breath from her. She stopped and stood motionless for a moment not knowing exactly what to do next. How could this stranger have found her and what in God's name could he want from her? Slowly the figure began to move out into the sunlight. It was then that Emma saw that it was not whom she had though it might be, but instead there was a man she had never seen before. He stood in the sunlight some 50 feet away just staring at her saying nothing. His stare was intent and he seemed as though he recognized her from somewhere. He stepped a few feet closer.

"What do you want?" Emma shouted nervously as she began walking towards him.

She decided she would confront this man and find out what it was he wanted. The man looked around as though surprised and frightened that she was approaching him. He took a few steps away, stumbling slightly. Emma could now see the fear in his face as she came closer to him.

"Who are you? What do you want with me?" Emma shouted at him now only 10, maybe 15 feet from the man.

As she continued to come closer to him, he suddenly raised up his arm. Emma could see that he was holding something. Before she could speak again, the man threw the object at her. Emma moved sharply to one side as the object

- 136 -

narrowly missed hitting her in the face. She turned abruptly as a brick smashed against the wall behind her and crumpled to the pavement in pieces. When she turned back towards the man, he had run off across the street and disappeared between two buildings.

"Hey you!" she shouted. "What the hell are you doing?"

She wanted to chase him down and smash him with the same brick he had just thrown at her. She felt a rage rise within her. Everything that was happening to her seemed to be attacking her sense of sanity. These people and this town are crazy, she thought…or was she?

As Emma turned and walked into the entrance of the motel, she looked through the window of the office and saw the old man standing there just staring at her. He had apparently seen everything, yet he did nothing. She stopped and stared back at him. He dropped his eyes and walked into the back room.

Once inside her motel room, Emma began shaking uncontrollably. The anger and the fear were all boiling over at once. In the past she only felt this way during and immediately after her worst nightmares, but now it seemed to consume her entire being. She reached for the table lamp on the nightstand.

Chapter Seven

Dr. Eugene Fischer had treated many patients who had suffered from psychosis of one sort or another and many neurological disorders over the years, but none had troubled him more than the nightmares he had encountered working with Emma Holcomb. The places and things she described were unsettling at best given that they seemingly had absolutely nothing to do with her rather ordinary life here in Glenhaven. He had sought to learn more about her childhood but found there were no records prior to her adoption. From everything he could learn about her after that fact, her life had been uneventful as far as any trauma or events that might give some indication as to where these nightmares she was having had come from. Over the months of seeing her, he had become increasingly concerned about her, partly because of the intensity of the increased occurrences of the nightmares and partly because of the feelings she was having about her husband seeming indifferent to the whole thing after so many years. It was bad enough that he wouldn't accept the incidents as being borne of some legitimate cause, but that he continually brushed them off by inferring that maybe his wife was just 'going crazy'. Even though he would always tell her that he was saying it in jest, it sometimes made Emma wonder.

Now, after having met with the authorities regarding his treatment of Emma, Dr. Fischer needed to talk with someone who he knew was close with Emma. He worried that she might be in trouble or in need of further intervention.

"Thank you so much for coming in to see me today Susan," Dr. Fischer said as he gestured for Susan to sit in the chair across from his desk.

As he sat down next to her in the other chair he continued.

"I'm only meeting with you today because I know you're the one who recommended me to her. I know you are her best friend and I'm hoping that you can talk with her about this situation."

Fischer went on to explain how he had been visited by Jim Burnside and his partner and how they had wanted to know whatever he could tell them about her mental state. He also explained what he had discovered regarding the medications he had prescribed for Emma.

"So let me understand this Gene, you prescribed medications for Emma 12 months ago and she never filled or renewed any of them?" Susan asked in amazement.

"I'm afraid so," he answered. "I checked with all the pharmacies in town and they never filled any of the orders I gave her. Can you talk with her and see what she's doing?"

"Gene, she's gone. Last week. She left on a trip. I haven't heard from her in days now," Susan explained.

"Where did she go? Can you reach her?" ee asked as he stood up and walked over to the window.

"I'm not sure where she was going," Susan answered. "The last time we spoke she wasn't really herself, doctor. In fact she was pretty nasty. She just said she had somewhere to go though she didn't know where it was or when she'd get there. Her behavior really has changed over the past few months. Ever since her nightmares started coming more frequently."

Staring out the window Dr. Fischer answered.

"I fear she may be a ticking time bomb."

Chapter Eight

As Emma stepped carefully through the partially opened door of her motel room into the afternoon daylight, she nudged the broken piece of wood back into her room and carefully closed the door. She walked over to her minivan and around it to see that the tire had been repaired. A note was placed between the wiper and her windshield. She reached for it and read that the tire had in fact been slashed and that the bill was waiting for her at the motel office. She got into the car and drove the short distance across the parking lot. When she entered the office no one was at the counter. Impatiently she patted the bell on the counter repeatedly until the young man appeared from the back room.

"I understand the bill for my tire is here," she said abruptly. "I'd like to pay for it now."

"Yes ma'am, it's right here," the young man replied reaching under a small stack of papers on the counter. "I figured you'd take care of it when you checked out," he added.

"Well, you figured wrong," she answered belligerently. "I'm not checking out and where is that old man?" she demanded. "I want to know why he slashed my tire!"

"Ma'am, that's my grandfather," the boy answered. "He didn't cut your tire. He wouldn't do a thing like that."

"Oh be quiet. You just tell him to stay out of my way."

As she turned to leave, Emma hesitated for a moment and reaching for the doorknob she turned and said;

"And have my room straightened while I'm out."

The young man stood in amazement as he watched

Emma walk to her car. He wondered if this was in fact the same woman he had spoken to this morning.

Emma arrived at the newspaper office shortly after 2 p.m.. She sat in her car looking at the large plate glass window before her. The name Joleyn Star was nearly half removed off the window from age. Established 1873 still barely visible under the name. The front door opened and out stepped the old man Pete Dougherty she had met earlier that day. He waved to Emma and gestured for her to come in. She opened the car door and stepped out.

"I hope this is a good time for you," she said as she made her way to the curb. "I don't want to bother you."

"Don't be silly, any time is okay. Not much happening right now anyway," Pete replied. "You're about the most exciting thing that's happened around here in a long time."

"I guess I'm lucky I'm here at all," she proclaimed as she sat down at the front counter. "Some weirdo tried to throw a brick at my face this morning after I left you," she continued. "I'm telling you there's some real strange people in your town."

"Are you kidding me? Why would anyone want to do that?" Pete exclaimed in shock. "What did he look like? Did you report it to the Sheriff?"

"No I didn't," Emma replied. "He was pretty strange though. He just kept staring at me like he knew me. He wouldn't answer me when I yelled at him and then he just hauled off and threw a brick at me. He was about my age I'd guess, real big heavyset guy with longish dirty brown hair and kind of a dumb look about him."

"Sounds like Kelly," Pete mused momentarily. "Nobody's sure if he's all there or not. Never says anything to anyone. Hasn't since he was a kid. Watched his mother get murdered when he was about four so I've heard. Must have traumatized him pretty bad. He's usually pretty harmless though. You got something about you missy that seems to be

- 141 -

stirring up a real hornets nest here."

Pete turned and picked up a whole stack of old newspapers from behind him and dropped them down on the counter in front of Emma.

"This'll get ya started. Pulled 'em from up in the attic. Goes back to around the time Flo's parents died. You might find what your looking for there."

"Thanks," Emma said as she reached for the first paper to start looking through.

"I'll be in the back room if you need me for anything. There's coffee over there," Pete said gesturing across the room to the table against the wall.

He walked through the archway to the back of the building where Emma could hear the sound of the presses running.

She really didn't know what she was looking for as she pored over page after page of old stories and pictures of people from another era. So what if she did find something relating to Flo or her parents. What would that prove? She didn't even know this woman and more importantly, Flo didn't know her.

Something however compelled her to keep looking. She had been at it for the better part of an hour and a half when she came upon a story that caught her eye. It seemed that two brothers, ages 8 and 12, were playing by the river just outside of town. Both had died that afternoon. One presumably by drowning, and the other by a seemingly bizarre event. It seemed, as the story went on, that the oldest boy was found dismembered several yards away in the woods. A bloodied ax was also found nearby leading the authorities at that time to conclude that they had both been murdered. But by whom remained unanswered.

Emma felt a warm flush come over her as she pushed her chair back from the counter. At first she thought she might faint and then that feeling gave way to nausea. Emma tried to stand but felt trapped as though straps were holding her arms to the chair. She couldn't move, but worse still, she couldn't speak. She sat there for several minutes staring down at the story. There it was in front of her. One of her darkest nightmares printed in black and white where anyone could see. Details that were only vague in her dreams were clearly described in the story before her. It had really happened and it happened here. Emma broke from the trance she had been in and abruptly stood up and walked across the room. She looked through the arch to the back room and saw Pete busily working at one of the presses. She felt panicked. On the one hand she wanted to run from this place and yet she felt as though she needed to stay and read more. Why, she did not know. She walked slowly back over to the counter, sat down and started turning pages again. The dates were not in perfect sequence but in a story she noted minutes later, she found something about a family that died in a fire at their home. The story went on to say that a local woman was suspected of setting the fire but that no one was able to prove it. The woman was never charged. Her name was not revealed in the story. The story made Emma feel extremely uncomfortable as she read on. At the bottom of the story was a place where there was a picture of the family that had died and the woman who had been suspected but the pictures had been cut out of the paper. Emma picked up the paper and walked through the archway to where Pete was working. She said nothing as he continued his work oblivious of her presence. Suddenly he turned and with a start, pushed the stop button on the press.

"You surprised me. I didn't know you were standing there," Pete said a bit shaken.

"Can you tell me why these pictures have been cut out of these papers?" Emma asked.

Pete reached over and took the page from Emma and glanced at the story she had just read.

"Can't say that I can," he replied. "There were quite a few pictures cut out of these old papers when I bought the place. Maybe someone was making an album? Did you find anything on Flo?" he asked.

"I'm not sure," Emma answered. "But I am finding some other stories that are rather disconcerting."

As the two of them stood there in the archway, the front door of the office swung open. Sheriff Wentworth and a deputy stepped in.

Emma and Pete both walked out into the front office. As they approached the counter the Sheriff spoke first.

"Ms Holcomb, I wonder if I could have a word with you,"

"How did you know I was here?" Emma asked.

"This is a small town ma'am, and your whereabouts seems to be a lot of peoples interest right now," the Sheriff answered.

Emma walked around the counter to face the two officers and said;

"What is it exactly you want to talk with me about Sheriff?"

"Can you tell us why you trashed your room over at the hotel?" the deputy asked.

"I did no such thing!" Emma exclaimed sitting back down in her chair. "Why would I tear up my own room?"

"That's what we were wondering," Sheriff Wentworth replied. "I figured with everything that went on this morning, you might have taken it out on your room."

Emma shot up out of her chair and leaned in towards the Sheriff.

"Well Sheriff, maybe you can tell me why the people in this town are treating me this way. First my tire is slashed. Then some crazy waitress goes off and hangs herself after seeing me in the restaurant. I mean, I know I don't look like much in the morning but this is ridiculous. Then some loony goes and throws a brick right at me and every time I see any old people in this town they either start whispering about me or they run off like they've seen a ghost or something. So you tell me, what's going on here in your quaint little town?"

"Lady, I don't really know," the Sheriff answered. "All I do know is that since you came into town last night you've been setting off fireworks all over the place. I'm gonna have to ask you to come with me over to the office for a little bit while I check a few things out."

"Are you arresting me?" Emma queried.

"No ma'am I'm not. I just need to verify who you are and where you came from."

"I told you all that this morning," Emma answered. "My husband died two months ago and I'm trying to put some of the pain behind by traveling some. I was a schoolteacher for years back in my town in Connecticut. I've lived there my whole life."

By now Emma's voice was shaking and she seemed to be growing hysterical as she continued.

"I have never been here before and I don't know any of these people. Why won't they just leave me alone?"

Emma paused for a moment and the Sheriff used the opportunity to take a step towards Emma to try and calm her if he could. Emma raised only her eyes towards the Sheriff. Her stare stopped him cold in his tracks.

"Where the hell am I?" Emma growled angrily.

"Look, I understand you're upset ma'am, but I still need to have you come over to the office with me," the Sheriff said.

As Emma took a step, the Sheriff and the deputy took a step back as though unsure of what she might do next. She turned towards Pete and said politely;

"How late will you be here? There are still some things I'd like to look at."

"I'll be here till six or seven. You come back when you're all done with the Sheriff," Pete replied.

Sheriff Wentworth walked over to the door and opened it waiting for Emma. She walked out into the sunlight.

"You can follow me over in your car if you like ma'am," the Sheriff said as he walked around the side of his truck and got in.

Emma opened the door to her minivan and before getting in, stopped and looked around. She felt as though there were hundreds of eyes upon her, but looking around she saw no one. She slid into the drivers seat, started her engine and followed the Sheriff down the street.

The deputy had remained behind and was asking Pete about Emma's interest in the old papers.

"I don't know," Pete said. "She's a little spooky. Seems awfully interested in people from way before her time. She's entitled to look if she wants though."

The deputy finished scribbling in his note pad and closed it up. He thanked Pete for his trouble and left the office. Pete watched him drive away. As he walked back to the counter he looked down at the papers Emma had left open. He turned a few pages when suddenly a story caught his eye. The heading read: *LOCAL WOMAN QUESTIONED IN DEATHS*. The caption under the accompanying picture went on to say that the woman pictured was the mother in the family that had been murdered in a fire. The story went on to say that the person suspected was never charged. The story stood out but it was the picture that sent goose bumps up and down Pete's arms. He reached up and removed his glasses, wiped them and returned them to his face as if to insure that he was seeing correctly. He leaned down and looked more closely at the picture. There in the picture was the woman identified as the deceased mother being covered up by someone. The lighting was obviously not the best for so old a camera, but the features were unmistakable. Pete expelled a quite whistle as he stared at the picture. What he was looking at seemed almost impossible considering the date of this story was some forty or more years ago, but unless he was going completely blind, the woman in the picture bore an uncanny resemblance to the woman who had been sitting in his office only moments before, but that was so long ago Pete thought.

He felt a shiver go up his spine. He looked around the dimly lit office as if to insure that no one else was watching. He slowly closed the paper.

Emma stepped out into the fading sunlight as the Sheriff held open the door to the Sheriff's station.

"I'm sorry we took as long as we did, but I really needed to understand a little more about you," he said as he escorted Emma to her car. "Since it's the weekend, I'll probably hear back from Connecticut on Monday. As far as your room goes, I'll talk to old man Tyler over at the hotel and work something out for you. Since it's the weekend, I'll probably hear back from your boss on Monday. Will you stay with us till then?"

Emma nodded affirmatively and got into her car. The Sheriff stood at her open window and gazing out over the roof of her car at the sinking sun added;

"Ya know, Flo's been around here for as long as anybody can remember, and even though her behavior hasn't always been easy to explain, what she did today really caught me off guard."

Emma repeated that she was at as much of a loss for an explanation as they all were.

"Oh, and about Kelly? I'll go have a talk with him too," the Sheriff added as Emma started up the car to leave.

As she started driving away from the Sheriff's station she though that she was really much to tired to go back to the paper today. What she really needed was something to eat and a good nights sleep. Hopefully this would be one of those nights her nightmares would stay away. As she pulled up in front of her room she saw that the room had been cleared out and the debris was piled up just outside against the wall. She glanced over at the office as she got out of her car and saw the old man standing at the window staring at her. She turned and went into her room to freshen up before going to get something to eat.

Emma went over to the diner where it had all begun this morning. As she entered a hush fell over the place as six or seven people that were in there turned to watch her walk in.

Obviously everyone knew about her or at least thought they did, but she didn't care now, and so she walked directly over to a booth and sat down. Sam came out from the back and walked over to her table and without asking sat down across from her. For a few moments they said nothing.

"I hear you ran into Kelly today," Sam began. "He's really a pretty harmless guy as a rule. He had to have been reacting to what happened to Flo. He's always been closer to her than anyone. You know he was there when his mother was killed.

"Yeah, I heard something like that," Emma sighed.

Sam turned his head and gazed out the window of the diner. He said nothing for several moments, then he spoke almost cautiously.

"Ya know," he began. "I've been sitting in this place for almost thirty years now and I've heard probably every lame story you can think of from almost everybody in this town. Who's sleeping with whom. Who's this one or that one is fighting with, and everything in between. If there's gossip to be told in this town, it's probably gonna be told right there at that counter. Some of the craziest stories come from some of the oldest folks here though."

Sam paused here for a long moment. It seemed to Emma that he really didn't want to tell her anymore.

"Well, you've certainly got my undivided attention. Do go on," she insisted.

"Well, most of it seems pretty far fetched," Sam began. "Apparently there was this family that lived here back in the late 30's, early 40's. In fact, their ancestors go back well into the 1800's. Anyway, story goes that they were as crazy as can be. Insane you know? Through the years there were reports of a whole lot of hanky panky going on within the family if you get what I'm saying," Sam turned back towards Emma and continued. "Mother and sons and I think even their little girl. They would do things around town that nobody could believe. The boys would kill neighbor's pets and hurt other children in

- 148 -

town. There was some talk that the daughter might have even killed some kids. Anybody that accused them of anything or picked on any of them or that the mother simply just didn't like, they'd usually end up hurt or even dead, usually in a real sick way too. No one could ever prove that she was the one doing it but amongst the oldest folks here there doesn't seem to be too much doubt."

As Emma sat listening, Sam continued.

"I remember Flo sitting right there at that counter telling me the strangest story one evening. As Flo told it, the mother was the strangest of them all. Apparently, there was this story about Kelly's mom; her name was Ruth, Ruth Walker. Supposedly one day as Kelly's mom, Ruth, went into the General store, she had noticed the old lady hunched over the counter and immediately began berating the woman for being there. At least that's how Flo heard it told. Anyway, I guess Ruth had pushed the woman aside as she went by saying how she couldn't understand why any store owner would even let her into their store. As she continued on through the store, the woman shook her fist and muttered something under her breath. Ruth turned and I guess the two women had words before the old woman mumbled some threat at Ruth, and shuffled out of the store. So then Flo told me that she learned that sometime during the middle of that same night, Ruth was woken up suddenly with a hand over her mouth. Apparently the old woman and her sons came calling. She was raped repeatedly in front of her small son and then dragged out of her house and tied to a tree where they slammed a car into her over and over until she was dead. They did it in front of her son. Can you believe that shit?" Sam said.

"The authorities found the car a week later. It had been set on fire, pushed over a cliff and destroyed. It turned out to have been stolen from a neighboring county a week before but its use was never known. Although many of the towns people suspected who had killed Ruth Walker, no one was able to prove that she or any of her sons were anywhere near Ruth's house that night, but it was the unspoken belief as to who was responsible. Again it appeared that they would get away with still another heinous act. Ruth's son, Kelly had been found the next day wandering around the property and was turned over to the state. It wasn't until he became of age that he returned here and lived mostly as a homeless person around town. He rarely let anyone come near him.

"Flo, and so many of the other town's folks grew increasingly frustrated at these people and their actions and finally decided that they alone must put and end to the insanity. She and three other locals drove the five miles out to where this woman lived with her four sons and one daughter conceived from one of her own sons. It was a full moon that night and it cast eerie shadows across the woman's property as they slowly pulled up in the middle of the night. Flo and the others walked silently across the field to the small farmhouse where they all were sleeping. Quietly, Flo and the others slipped inside the house. Flo, lifted the young girl up from where she lay sleeping, covering the little girl's mouth. She carried her out of the house while the others ever so quietly poured gasoline from the cans they had carried in, up and down the hallways and on the walls of the small dwelling. As the last one left, they set the place ablaze. As they walked silently away from the house, Flo turned and walked over to the well nearby and without a moment's hesitation, lifted the child and threw her down into the darkness of the well. They all stood and watched as the house burned.

"As the volunteer firemen arrive, they watched as the men were forced back time and again, preventing them from going inside to try and save anyone. Finally two firemen were able to get in through a fallen wall on the side of the house and return dragging one body out. It was the mother. Flo and her accomplices rushed over to see if she has survived. Her body was charred and still smoking as they looked down upon her. She seemed to be dead when suddenly from deep within her body came a sickening scream yealling; "My girl, my baby, they've killed my girl. The well, the well." One of the firefighters turned and ran over to the well. He shined his flashlight down into the well and shouted back to the others to give him a hand, then using ropes and lowering one of the men into the well, they were able to retrieve the young girl and although bruised and broken, she seemed as though she may be okay.

"The scorched woman laying on the ground although in her final throws of death, looked abruptly up at Flo and the others and from deep within her seared lungs she musters a frightening sound threatening them, saying; "she'll get you for this. One day she'll get you for this." Flo and the others just stood in terror as the firemen wrapped the girl in blankets and handed her to the ambulance attendants for the trip to the hospital."

Sam stared out the window again for a long time before finishing.

"Flo seemed to be always looking over her shoulder as long as I've known her."

Sam turned and looked back at Emma. Emma didn't say a word, nor did she even look at Sam as she got up and left the diner. She didn't even get her car, but instead walked the block and a half back to the hotel. As she entered the overhang, she noticed the old man standing in the darkened office just staring at her. She stopped and stared back at him for several minutes. Then smiling, she turned and walked across the parking lot to her room.

Emma's eyes bolted open with a start. She lay there for several moments unsure if she was having another one of her nightmares or if she was really awake. Suddenly she heard a loud crackling sound and glass breaking. As she glanced over at the closed curtains it seemed as though it were much to bright out for the hour that shone clearly on the clock next to her bed. She slowly rose from her disheveled bedding and stepping over the covers on the floor, walked to the window. As she drew the curtain back she could now see it all quite clearly. The office of the hotel was completely engulfed in flames. No fire crews had arrived yet. Half asleep guests were gathering in the parking lot in front of her room. She could here them frantically talking among themselves wondering if anyone could have survived it since it went up so fast.

Emma let the curtain drop and walked slowly back over to the bed. She reached down and picked up the blanket off the floor. She had to get some sleep she thought.

As the sun rose over the hills just outside of town, a plain green sedan slowly turned the corner onto the main street. The two men seated inside, silhouetted against the early morning sun behind them sat silently as they rolled up the main street and parked in front of the Sheriff's office. Around the corner and only blocks away, the burned and twisted remains of the hotel office lay smoldering as the firemen lifted the wrapped bodies of the only two victims they found into the back of the black station wagon.

Two vehicles turned into the parking lot and made their way across the lot to park side by side in front of Emma's room. The doors of the vehicles opened and out stepped two men from the sedan and one man from the truck. The parking lot was covered in water and one man reached down to brush off a wet piece of paper that had attached itself to the side of his snakeskin boot. They walked up to the motel room door and knocked. After there was no immediate answer, one of the men knocked again. This time harder and shouts out.

"Emma Holcomb, this is the police. Please open your door."

After a few moments the door slowly opens and Emma sees a familiar face. It's Jim Burnside and his partner. As the three men move into the room forcing Emma back, Jim Burnside speaks first.

"Ms. Holcomb, your under arrest for the murder of your

husband. You have the right to remain silent. If you give up that right, anything you say can and will be used against you in a court of law. You have the right to an attorney. If you cannot afford one at this time, one will be appointed for you. Do you understand these rights as I have explained them to you?"

Emma just smiled and said wryly;
"But I'm not done with my vacation."

THE END

Tales from the Mind Field

DEAD END

By
R.M.Villoria

Chapter One

I'm not sure exactly what it was that woke me that night, the thunder, the sound of the rain on the roof, or the wind as it brushed the limbs across the eave of the patio, but as I lay there in a half sleep half awake state, I felt myself get up and walk over to my dresser. I picked up my pen that I usually had there and wrote something down on the opened envelope lying nearby in the dim light. I turned and shuffled back over to the bed and lay back down.

When I awoke the next morning, I knew I had gotten up for something during the night but I couldn't remember what it was for. I rose and looked out the window. The storm had passed and the skies were clearing. *It was going to be a nice day*, I thought.

I turned and shuffled off to the bathroom to get ready for work. *Can't wait for Saturday,* I thought as I turned the shower knobs.

When I finished dressing I walked over to my dresser to grab my watch and wallet. It was only then that I noticed the folded empty envelope with the writing on it. I remembered now. I had gotten up during the night and come over here to write something down. *What was it though?*

I picked up the paper and read it.

4766 Dillard Rd.

Weird, I thought. *Why would I write down an address I had never heard of before?* I didn't remember dreaming anything about an address. I glanced at my watch and saw that I was already behind schedule. Tossing the envelope back down on the dresser, I thought; *I'll have to grab some coffee on the way in*. I hurried out the front door to work.

As he drove he couldn't help but continue to think, why had he written down that address last night?

As he usually did on mornings when he was late, John stopped by the local donut shop to grab a cruller and a cup of coffee on the way into the office.

"Hi John, how are you this morning," the cheerful voice rang out from behind the counter.

John was late often enough that the girl behind new him pretty well.

"Hi Beth," John answered. "Not bad for a Wednesday. I'll have my usual please."

As Beth reached into the case for the donut, John poured himself a cup of coffee in one of the Styrofoam cups on the counter. As he added the sugar and milk he paused for a moment and asked;

"Hey Beth, let me ask you something. Have you ever heard of a Dillard Road?"

"Doesn't ring a bell off hand," she answered as she handed him his cruller.

Another patron had entered the establishment and Beth turned to him and asked.

"Have you heard of a Dillard Road anywhere around here?"

The man thought about it for a moment and answered; "Nah, haven't."

"Why?" Beth asked as John reached over the counter and handed her his money for the food and coffee.

"Strangest thing," he responded. "I wrote it down in my sleep last night. I have no idea why." He turned and walked towards the exit.

"Well, if you find a million dollars there, remember who your friends are," Beth laughingly called out as John walked out of the shop.

As John sat down at his desk and began looking over the reports that were left over from the previous day, all thoughts of the address and the night before left his mind. In fact, John forgot all about the address over the next two days and paid the folded envelope on his dresser no attention at all.

Here it was 1985 and he still had reports from late '84 on his desk that hadn't been resolved yet. He didn't want to ask for assistance but he was beginning to feel like this was going to get the better of him. He poured all his attention into the work for the rest of the week.

On Saturday, John woke up late and as he lay there thinking about what he wanted to do that day, he remembered the address on the envelope still sitting on the dresser. He got up and walked over to pick it up. He sat down on the end of the bed and just stared at the address. Was it someplace he'd been, he wondered. Had he been dreaming about an account from work and maybe just remembered an address he saw on a form there? It didn't sound familiar as he repeated it to himself. As he tossed it back up on the dresser, he figured he'd look it up on the map on his office wall. With that, slipped on his shorts to get the day started.

John walked into the kitchen and pushed the on button to the coffee maker. As he stood there gazing out the window waiting for the coffee maker to warm up he noticed the mailman walking up the street. If anyone would know where that address was, surely Roger, the mailman would. Reaching over the sink and sliding the window open, John shouted out to the mailman.

"Hey Roger, come here a minute would you?"

Roger turned and walked across the grass to the window where John was waiting.

"Roger, have you ever heard of Dillard Road?" John asked through the open window.

Roger thought for several moments as though trying to recollect everywhere he had been.

"No, Davis Road. There's a Davis Road on the east side of town. I've never delivered there but I have seen stuff addressed there."

"No, I think I'm looking for a Dillard Road," John answered.

"Sorry I couldn't be more help," Roger said as he tipped his hat and continued on his route.

"Thanks anyway," John shouted after him.

John poured himself a cup of the now ready coffee and sat down at the kitchen table. *Maybe I can find it in the phone book,* he thought.

After several unsuccessful attempts at trying to find the street name in the phone book, John simply gave up and decided to go for a run instead. Changing into some running shorts and a tank top, he headed out the door and down to the park where he normally worked out with his weekend jog. All the while as he ran around the lake and through the trails at the park, this morning he could not shake the idea of finding the address that for some unknown reason he had written down in a half sleep last week. It was crazy he thought, but now he had an idea, and so after his run and after he had gone home and cleaned up, he called an old friend of his that worked at one of the county offices. He was certain that he would be able to find out where that address was.

"Hank? Hi Hank, it's John," he spoke into the phone. "I need your help with something and I wondered if you might be available this afternoon."

Hank was a county engineer and so John figured if he could take a look at the county maps, maybe the address would show up on there.

"Sure John, what do you need?" Hank answered.

"Well, I was wondering if I could meet you down at your office and try to find an address on one of those county maps."

"Today? It's Saturday John, what's so important that you need it today?"

John explained how this address came to be and how he really wasn't available during the week and so on and so forth until finally Hank agreed to meet him in twenty minutes down at his office.

"Thanks Hank, I appreciate it," John replied. He walked out to his car and headed for the county offices.

They met out in front of the offices and for the next thirty minutes Hank and John poured over several maps in the office looking for Dillard Road. Suddenly Hank called John over to one of the maps he had pulled out and was looking at.

"Here you go John, here's an entry showing a Dillard Road way out south of town. This is an old map though so I can't guarantee that it even exists anymore. That's all open land out there."

John studied the map and saw how he could access that road by going down one road and over to another. He wrote down his own directions and patting his friend on the back said;

"Thanks a million Hank," as he headed out the door.

As he drove out of the parking lot he thought; *why not take the time this afternoon and see what was at the address.* He headed down the highway towards the south end of town. What would he find there? Who would he find there? Was there something significant there that would affect him personally? Several questions kept rolling around in his head as he drove.

It took nearly forty minutes to get into the area and after several wrong turns and a back track or two, John came across a half dirt and half paved road that seemed to appear out of nowhere. He almost passed it and stopped and backed his car up slowly. Most of the blacktop had eroded away. The sloped curbs were either broken or non-existent. He stopped the car, got out and looked around for any signage that would indicate if this was the right place. There were several old homes down the length of the road to a curve almost a quarter of a mile away where he couldn't see any further. As he walked to the side of the road he noticed an old wooden street sign laying on the ground almost obscured by the over growth. With his foot he brushed away some of the growth. It read Dillard Rd. He pulled it out from under the weeds and left it by the side of the road. John returned to his car and proceeded slowly.

He strained to find numbers on the first few houses that he saw. Some of the numbers were also barely visible on the sloped curbs. 10166, 10159, it appeared that this was going to be a fairly long road as he continued driving. The houses grew farther apart after he passed the curve and the numbers decreased more quickly. 8993, 8754, 7500 now the houses were not only a good distance apart, but also most of them looked as though they had stood empty for quite some time.

Boarded up windows, shoulder high weeds and dead trees all seemed to indicate that this end of Dillard Road had been abandoned years ago. The lots were one and two acres in size and the homes were clearly built many years before.

He read the barely visible numbers...6122, 5955, and then suddenly there was nothing. Nothing at all, no homes, no lot boundaries, nothing to indicate where 4766 might be. Just open areas with weeds, more dead trees but no homes anywhere.

Ahead, the road, which now had now pretty much turned to nothing more than dirt, looked to come to an end. John proceeded very slowly. He noticed that on one or two of the curbs before him were the faded numbers where homes might at one time have been. 4780... across the road he could barely make out 4769. He got out of the car and walked to where he thought 4766 should be. He brushed aside dried dirt and weeds on the broken concrete curb. There it was, barely visible…4766.

It was nothing more than a huge lot with more overgrown weeds, a few trees that were dead for some time but nothing more, no home, no building of any sort. Not even an old foundation where a building might have stood at one time. John walked into the open space and thought. *What could possibly cause him to get up from his sleep and write down this address when there clearly was nothing here?*

John stood there for several minutes looking around for anything that might give him a clue as to why he was there, but there was nothing, not even the sound of a bird. As he turned to leave, he noticed another car slowly pulling up behind his own. He stopped and watched a woman get out. She was maybe in her thirties and was looking around as if lost. John called out to her as he walked back towards the cars.

"Looking for something?" he asked.

The woman came around in front of her car and spoke fairly softly.

"Well, I'm a little embarrassed to say this, but I was looking for an address out here."

"Really, why?" John asked.

"Well, you probably won't believe me if I tell you but, about two weeks ago I woke up in the middle of the night, at least I think I woke up, and I wrote this address down. It was 4766 on this road. I didn't really give it a lot of thought but since I wasn't doing anything today I thought I'd try to find it. Is this it? I must have asked twenty different people if they knew where it was. Finally one old man at the hardware store said he thought it might be down this way. Once I got down this far I figured I'd keep looking. I saw the sign laying by the side of the road and decided I might as well continue," the woman paused for a moment and then continued. "I have to say, I was actually a little frightened to come out here. I didn't know what I would find."

John didn't make a sound. Instead he just stood staring at this woman. His thoughts came fast. *Was she kidding? Had she really done the exact same thing he had done in the middle of the night? Had she really written down the very same address?*

"What's wrong?" she asked as she took a step back. "Why are you staring at me that way? You're making me a little nervous."

"I'm sorry," John blurted out. "I didn't mean to upset you but I mean this is crazy! It just can't be. I also wrote down this address in my sleep just last week. I have no idea why, but I too decided to come out here today and see if I could figure what the heck it's all about."

They both stood silent for several moments looking around as if hoping no one had overheard their preposterous stories. They both returned looking at each other in disbelief. A hundred questions seemed to race through their heads. *Had they known someone who lived here? Had they been here before, maybe as children? Who or what would cause two complete strangers to be drawn to the same address at around the same time?*

"I'm sorry, my name is John. Yours?"

"Susan," she replied. "What do you suppose we should do about this?"

They decided that they would go to John's friend's office the following week and see if they could find out any more information about this particular plot of land.

They traded phone numbers and agreed to call each other during the week to make the arrangements.

John was still curious though as he drove home. He wanted to see if there was anyone else he knew that might know something about this address. He decided to stop by his Mom's place on the way home. He remembered that she had a neighbor who was at least 88-years-old and he figured if anyone might know something, it might be him. As far as John could remember, he thought the old guy's name was Gus and he lived there pretty much alone. His daughter came by often

- 162 -

to check on him but as far as he knew, this guy Gus was still pretty self-sufficient.

As he pulled into his mother's driveway he noticed the old guy sitting on his front porch. Instead of going in to greet his mom, John went directly over to the old man and walked up onto the porch.

"Hi there," John began. "I don't know if you remember me or not but I'm Beverly's son, John from next door?"

"Well hey there young man," the old guy replied. "What brings you over here today? Fine woman your mother is, and a mighty fine baker too I'd guess from the smells coming from that kitchen window. Why I almost got up the nerve a while back to go on over there and ask for some pie."

John half laughed, smiled and answered;

"I'm sure my mom would have been delighted to give you some of her baking. She would have loved the company too."

John's dad had passed away eight years earlier from colon cancer and he knew his mother would probably have welcomed another person to talk with. She didn't go out much anymore and he didn't get over there as often as he or she would have liked.

"So tell me, what can an old cuss like me do for you today?"

John sat down next to the old man in the other chair and began;

"Well...is it Gus?"

The old man nodded yes.

"Well Gus, I was wondering if you knew about any of the old roads around town maybe from years ago. The one I'm interested in is called Dillard Road. It's on the south end of town about eight or so miles past the old rubber factory."

The old man rubbed his fingers back and forth across the stubble on his chin a bit as if to contemplate the question.

"You know my memory just isn't what it used to be. I might have driven on that road as a young man like you but I just don't remember. South of town you say?"

John nodded.

The old man sat back in his chair and gazed out across his front lawn. He didn't say anything for a good minute or two and then a sign of recollection came over his wrinkled face.

"Used to be a big old scary house out that way I think when we were kids. Use to ride our bikes all the way out there. Threw rocks at the windows. Folks used to say that there was a witch living there but I never saw her. In fact now that I'm thinking about it, I don't remember seeing anybody living there. You thinking about buying some land out there?" the old man asked.

John decided it would probably be better if he didn't go into the reasons for his inquiry.

"No, I was just curious about some of the older areas of town," John answered.

"Funny," the old man continued half laughing. "Some days I can remember all kinds of things from way back when, but I'll be darned if I can remember what I had for breakfast on any given day."

John smiled and stood up.

"Well Gus, I want to thank you for letting me chat with you today."

"That's okay son, glad to help. And you say hi to your mom for me and tell her I think her kitchen smells real good."

John smiled and walked off the porch and across the lawn to his mother's house.

As he walked in the front door he called out to his mother.

"Mom. You here?"

"In the kitchen John," He heard her reply.

Gus was right. The smell of her baking something permeated the entire house. It smelled great John thought.

"And to what do I owe this pleasure?" she continued.

"Actually, I just stopped by to talk with your neighbor."

"Gus?" she asked.

"Yeah, I was curious if he knew any of some of the old roads from awhile back here in town."

"Was he able to help you?" Beverly asked.

"Kind of, but not really," John answered as he watched his mother pulling a baked pie out of the oven.

"Why are you looking for old roads?" she asked.

"Well mom, you probably will think I'm crazy but..." John proceeded to tell her all about the dream, if it was one, and the address and what had happened today and the woman he met there with the very same story.

"Well," she began. "You be careful. There hasn't been any activity out that way for a very long time. I remember your father used to go out to the rubber factory when he needed things for his shop. They built a development south of there but it never really took off. Only a handful of homes were sold and most of those people moved away shortly after buying."

"Why was that?" John asked curiously as he tried to pick a piece of crust off the pie his mother had just baked.

Lightly smacking his hand in disapproval, she responded;

"Nobody really knew. It was kind of a mystery. People moved in and then they moved right out shortly after. Nobody seemed to stay out there very long. There were lots of rumors and lots of stories. There was this one story that I remember from back in high school about a family that moved in out there years before. Nice family I think I remember it said. Anyway, they disappeared one day shortly after they moved into a house way out there, just vanished. Most folks believed they must have moved away in the middle of the night. Maybe they didn't pay their mortgage or something I don't know, but they left everything behind, all their furniture, clothing, everything. It was very strange."

"Didn't anybody look for them?" John asked.

"I don't know, I never heard."

John got up to leave.

"I gotta get going," he said as he kissed his mom on the

cheek and headed for the door.

"By the way, you ought to take a piece of that pie next door to old man Gus. He lusts after the smells from your cooking."

Beverly laughed as John closed the door behind him and walked out to his car.

Chapter Two

Monday morning was Margie Reinhart's time for doing laundry though today she wasn't sure if she would make it through all three loads. She was just putting the second load in the dryer when a wave of fatigue came over her. She hadn't slept well the last two nights and now she felt like just lying down and taking a nap. 11:37 on the kitchen clock, the kids wouldn't be home from school for several hours and she really needed the sleep. A short nap wouldn't hurt she thought as she walked into the bedroom.

2:23 Margie saw on the bedside clock. *Oh my God* she thought as she sat up on the bed *that was the weirdest dream I've ever had.*

She couldn't believe she had slept that long and now it was panic time to get ready and go pick up the kids at school. She leapt up off the bed and walked over to her dressing table. She had always wanted a formal dressing table with a chair and a mirror like her mother had. They had found this one at an auction a few years back and with a little love and a coat of paint had made it into exactly what she had wanted. Now, as she sat down to put a brush through her hair, she felt goosbumps crawl up her arm and a cold chill swept over her. She stared at the mirror in disbelief. There scrawled on the mirror in her own handwriting with her red lipstick was; "4766 Dillard Rd."

What was this? Some joke someone had played on her? Had someone come in the house while she was sleeping and done this?

She didn't have time to give it much thought. She had to get to the school and pick up her children. She would deal with this later.

That evening when her husband Rick came through the front door from work, Margie was waiting for him.

"Hi sweetheart. How are..." He stopped cold and saw his wife just standing there with this blank stare on her face. "What's wrong Margie, you look like you've just seen a ghost. Come over here and sit down."

"No," she replied and without speaking a word reached for Rick's hand and led him up the stairs to their bedroom.

When they entered the room Margie simply pointed at the mirror. Rick walked over and looking at the address scrawled on the mirror asked;

"What's this?"

"I don't know," she said. "I laid down for a nap this morning and when I woke up a couple of hours later, it was there. I think I got up in my sleep and wrote it. It's my handwriting. But I have no idea why I did it or where it is."

"You probably just had a bad dream," Rick offered in an almost dismissive manner.

"I don't think so," she replied. "When I went and picked the kids up today from school, I overheard Ms. Cunningham from the school office telling one of the parents that she had done the very same thing two nights ago. She got up in her sleep or so she thought and wrote down that address on a piece of paper. It gave me the chills Rick. I'm a little scared."

"I'll tell you what," Rick offered. "How about if I call the police station and talk with them and see if there's been some burglaries around town and if this fits in. Would that make you feel a little better?"

Margie answered that it would and went downstairs to start dinner.

About twenty minutes later, Rick came into the kitchen

and sat down at the counter. He just stared out the window without saying a word.

"Did you call the police?" Margie asked. "What did they say?"

Rick looked back at Margie and began to speak.

"Apparently there have been a bunch of other reports of this very same thing happening to different people around town over the last three weeks. They said a couple of folks even went out and found this address way out at the south end of town. They didn't find anything though, just an empty field. Frankly sweetie, I don't know what to tell you."

After that, Rick didn't give the matter much more thought. But it continued to bother Margie.

The next day after dropping the kids off at school, Margie drove over to the local precinct station to talk with the police. After waiting for twenty minutes or so, an officer led her to a small office in the corner of what appeared to be the squad room. A large burly plain clothed officer entered and sat down across from her at a table.

"So Ms. Reinhart is it?" he began. "I'm Sergeant Wilcox and I've been asked to look into these occurrences that have been happening to some of the people here in town. Your husband called here last night reporting that someone may have entered your home during the day and written an address on your mirror? Do I have that right?"

Margie acknowledged that his information seemed correct and added;

"But it seems to be happening to other people also. Why would anyone do this?"

"Well, frankly ma'am, we have no information that would lead us to believe that there is any one or more people entering homes during the day or night and writing this address down. We sent two officers out to that address this morning and they found absolutely nothing there. It's a big empty lot. If it's kids pulling a prank, we can't figure out how they're getting into some of these homes."

Margie sat for several moments and finally said;

"I'm a little frightened of all this."

"Well," Wilcox said as he got up from across the table "I wouldn't worry too much about it if I were you. It's probably nothing more than a coincidence, a fairly large coincidence, but nevertheless not something too serious. We'll let you know if we come up with anything that's pertinent that you should know about okay?"

Margie got up and shook the officers hand. Thanking him she walked out of the police station no less confused over the whole matter as she was when she entered.

John picked up the ringing phone at his desk just as he was getting ready to leave for lunch.

"John? It's Hank. Hey I really didn't want to bother you at work but I was wondering something," he asked.

"Hey, what's up Hank? I was gonna call you this week about that address I got from you."

"John, that's exactly what I'm calling you about. Did you ever find that address you were looking for?" Hank asked.

"Actually, yes I did. It turned out to be nothing though. Just an big empty lot. Didn't look as if anything or anybody had ever been there. Funny thing happened though, while I was there, another gal pulled up looking for the same address. Said she wrote it down just like I did. In a dream sort of. Weird eh?"

"John if you're standing up I think you should sit down."

"Okay, you've piqued my interest, what gives?" John answered as he sat back down at his desk.

"There have been eight of them," Hank answered almost in a whisper.

"Eight what?" John asked.

Hank continued although John could tell by the

trepidation in his voice that the information he was about to convey was going to call into question his own sanity.

"Eight more people have come in here looking for that same address. They all say they saw it in a dream like state just like you and got out of bed and wrote it down."

"Are you kidding me Hank? Eight more people have come in and asked you to see those maps to find that address?"

There were several seconds of complete silence.

"Yes, and they all want to go out there to find out if there's anything credible about it. Some of them are painting a picture of doom and gloom while some of them think they're going to find a pot of gold out there. I guess some of them have gone to the police about it."

"What can the police do?" John asked.

"I don't know," Hank replied.

John could feel the uneasiness in Hanks voice clear through the phone. There had to be a scientific explanation for so many people having the same dreams as he had.

"I'm gonna call Sheriff Franks this afternoon and see if maybe he has some idea of what's going on," Hank said. "It's probably nothing, but just the same, it sure is an interesting coincidence."

"Okay, you do that and let me know what he says," John answered.

John slowly hung up the phone and sitting there for a few moments started wondering what sinister thing was going on in this town now that as many as eight other people had been into the county offices looking for that same address. John was now more curious than ever to find out as much as possible about this address that seemed to be appearing to so many people in town. He decided to call the woman he had met out there and see if she wanted to join him in his further inquiry. He pulled the folded up paper out of his wallet and reached for the phone on his desk.

"Hello Susan?" he asked as she answered. "This is John. We met out at Dillard Road a few weeks ago?"

"Oh, hi John," Susan answered. "How are you?"

"Well, right now just a little freaked out," John said. "It seems that there are people all over town experiencing the very same thing you and I did."

"What, you mean the address?" she asked.

"Yeah, and apparently they all have the same story about getting up from their sleep and writing it down," John continued. "Apparently quite a few of them have gone down to the county office looking for directions."

"Should we go to the police?" Susan asked.

"We could," John answered. "But I was thinking more along the lines of getting all of these folks and us together and see what might be a common denominator among us. I mean there's got to be a reason why we all are being directed to this place don't you think?"

"Yeah," Susan answered tentatively.

"I'm gonna see if I can get the names and phone numbers of these other people and I'll call you back," John offered.

In a weakened voice Susan answered;

"Okay."

John hung up the phone and immediately called his friend Hank back at the county office.

"Hank? It's John again. Did any of those people have to sign in on that log you keep every time someone asks to see county maps?"

After a moment of silence, Hank answered.

"Yeah, they all did."

"Hank, I need that list. I want to talk with them and see if any of us have anything in common besides this address," John said.

"Okay John, it's yours."

John hung up the phone and grabbing his jacket rushed out of the office. As he passed his secretary he said;

"Cancel any other appointments I have today Judy."

At home that afternoon with the list, John called each of the names on the sheet and talked briefly with each of them. They all agreed it would be a good idea to get together and so John arranged for a meeting with them all for the following week at his home. He called Susan and told her of the meeting and she agreed to come as well.

It was a Thursday night and as was often the case this time of year, the weather had turned suddenly. The rain had begun around noon and had only gotten stronger as the evening progressed. The storm was now in full swing with continued thunder and lightning. The winds were now making it harder to see as John looked out his front window for the lights from any of the cars that should be arriving within the next fifteen minutes or so. Hopefully at least some of the people who had agreed to come would show up. It probably wasn't the best night to be gathering to talk about so eerily a coincidence as this was.

Within the hour, first one, then another until ten other people who had experienced this phenomenon arrived. Surely the curiosity alone had brought them all out this night. Through the evening each one related how they had come to write down the address. Although the evening did bring together people who might never have met before and in some small way kindle some friendships, it never revealed anything that would connect any of these people to the address or each other.

Everyone left that night with no more feeling of resolution than when they had arrived. The one thing that was agreed upon was that perhaps they should all go out to the location together at some time. They all would work with each other's schedule to see when they could arrange the time.

Three weeks later on a Saturday morning, John arose early. This was the day that they would all meet at 4766 Dillard Road. *Perhaps,* he thought, *if everyone is all there together some answer might be found.* John got up and dressed and went out to the kitchen to make coffee. As he waited, he called Susan to see if she was ready to go ahead and meet him out there. While on the phone they both confided in each other that they didn't sleep all that well the night before in anticipation of today's meeting. John didn't think it would be all that different from the day he and Susan had first met out there but still there was an uneasy feeling in the air that morning. John left his house at 9:30 that morning to meet with all the others at the location.

Chapter Three

Spenser looked at the clock on the wall. It read 10:15. Monday morning and already after ten o'clock he thought, John was never late for the monthly management meeting. He knew his co-worker had put in a lot of hours getting those reports up to date and he also knew that John wanted to be able to show that he'd been able to do it without any assistance.

"Where's John?" someone asked as they all sat around the conference table.

Spenser answered that he didn't know but that he'd go back to his office and call his house just to make sure he hadn't over slept or if he was perhaps already on his way. Some of the staff got up to pour another cup of coffee or grab another donut while they waited. Five minutes passed and Spenser came back into the room.

"No answer," he reported.

"Well, let's get started," someone said. "John will just have to catch up when he gets here."

The meeting lasted about an hour and a half. John never did make the meeting.

Spenser said he would call John's house again. By mid-afternoon when no one had heard from John, Spenser asked John's secretary if she had heard from him at all. When she said she hadn't, Spenser began to wonder about him. He and John had worked together on several projects over the years and so they had developed a simple friendship though it never had gotten social to where they would do anything together outside of work, still Spenser was a little concerned that his fellow worker had simply not come in today or even called with a reason. *Oh well,* he thought. He was sure John would explain tomorrow when he came in.

Tomorrow and the next day came and went, and John still had made no appearance at work. Concerned, John's secretary said she thought it might be a good idea to call the police and see if maybe he had been in an accident or something.

"Surely they would have that type of information," she offered to the others standing at her desk.

The officer on the other end of the phone listened intently as Judy, John's secretary, related how John had now missed three days work and that repeated calls to his house had gone unanswered. She told him how someone from the office had even gone by his place that morning but his car was not there and neither was he.

After taking the information from her and filling in the report, the desk officer turned to his boss, Sheriff Franks, there in the station and said;

"Now this is weird sir."

Franks and Sergeant Wilcox were both together at Wilcox's desk as the officer spoke.

"How's that?" he answered looking up from his work to address the officer.

"This has got to be at least the eighth or ninth call in here to report somebody missing. I've got a whole list here," the officer said waving a sheet of paper in front of him.

"Really?" the Sheriff responded. "Over how long a period?"

"Since Saturday night," the officer answered.

"Let me see that list," he said as he got up from his desk and walked over to the officer's desk.

Sheriff Franks looked over the list intently for some time and then dropping the paper back on the officers desk, barked out an order.

"I want a car out to everyone on that lists home right now! I'll take the Reinhart woman. Wilcox, you're with me."

The two men rushed out of the office. The officer looking at the list suddenly had a look of recognition on his face. He began dispatching units.

It had now been nearly 36 hours since Rick Reinhart had come into the station to report his wife's disappearance.

He related to Sheriff Franks and Sergeant Wilcox as they stood on the front porch how he was frantic with worry and had even suggested that they look into some of the people she had visited with a few weeks earlier. Franks wanted to know more about the meeting his wife had attended and who was there.

Rick had to honestly say that he didn't know too much about it except that they were supposedly all involved in a matter concerning some address.

Leaving the Reinhart residence, Sheriff Franks called the one person he knew had been in contact with most if not all of these people.

Hank answered the phone in his office.

"Hi Sheriff, what's up?" he asked.

"You know all those people who were coming by your office to find that address out on the south end of town? Well, it seems like there all missing over the past couple of days. How about grabbing that map and coming with me. Thought we might take a ride out there."

"Sure," Hank replied. "When?"

"Right now, I'll be by in about ten minutes," the sheriff replied.

After picking up Hank, Sheriff Franks asked him;

"What's that address they had all been talking about?"

"4766 Dillard Road," Hank answered.

Franks turned the cruiser and turning on his lights and siren, they sped towards the south end of town. He finally found the road and they proceeded slowly past the curve. As they continued he saw well ahead of them what appeared to be a number of cars parked on both sides of the road. Pulling up he expected to see the group of people somewhere nearby. The three men got out of the car and stood there looking at all the parked cars. Sheriff Franks walked by several of them. The keys were not in the ignition on any of them.

"Keys in any of those?" he shouted to Hank on the other side of the road.

"No, none," Hank replied.

Wilcox added;

"None here either."

The three men walked onto the lot and looked around. They saw nothing and heard nothing. They saw no one anywhere as far as they could see. Not a sound. Just eleven cars parked out on the street. The two men stayed out there for the better part of an hour walking around staring out at nothing.

"Where do you suppose they went?" Hank asked Sheriff Franks.

"I don't know. People just don't disappear into thin air," he answered.

"Let's bring the chopper out here boss and take a broader look at the area," Wilcox suggested. "Maybe they wandered off a good distance."

"Okay," the sheriff said. "Go on back to the car and call it in."

Susan touched John's arm and asked again;

"Why can't they see us John?"

John looked straight at Sheriff Franks, waved his arms and yelled. He turned to Susan and answered.

"They can't hear us either. It's like we're here, but were not."

Several of the others were now becoming somewhat panicked, as they too couldn't seem to communicate with the three men who had arrived over an hour ago. Trying to return to their cars, each of them was stopped by something invisible that seemingly wouldn't allow them to walk off the property.

"This guy just walked right through me!" one of the eleven yelled out. "What the hell is going on here!?"

The search went on for hours, days and even months. To this day not one of those eleven people had ever been seen or heard from again. They never were able to explain it

Bradley excitedly opened the box containing his new Smartphone. This new phone was amazing he thought. The features were far more superior to his older model. The screen clarity alone made it possible to see so much more clearly. The maps, the camera and the availability of so many more apps. He sat down at the table at Starbucks to start configuring the new phone. The time was set 3:37 and today's date was correct. Tuesday, May 14, 2014. He set the sound effects for incoming calls and text messaging. His girlfriend

Mary called out to him as she ordered their drinks.

"Do you want whipped cream on yours Brad?"

"No," was all he said as he continued playing with his new phone.

"Hey Brad, what do ya wanna do for dinner tonight?" she asked.

"Um, I don't know. How about that new Mexican spot. Rosita's I think it's called," he answered not looking up from his new "toy".

"I don't know, I guess. Where is it?" she asked.

"I think it's near downtown on Chandler somewhere," Bradley answered. "I'll look it up on my phone later."

As Mary sat down across from Brad placing their drinks down, she reached over to touch his hand.

"Brad, there's something I want to talk to you about," she began.

Brad set his new phone down on the table and looked up at her.

"Okay, what?" he answered a little concerned.

"Oh," she answered. "It's not that serious. I just wanted to talk about me moving in with..." Mary's comments were suddenly interrupted by the sound of Brad's phone. It was the tone he had set for receiving text messages.

"That's weird," he said as he reached for the phone. "I haven't given anyone this new number yet."

He swiped the screen and opened the message. It read that it was from an unknown sender. The text message simply read...**4766 Dillard Rd.**

THE END

Tales from the Mind Field

THE AGENT
By
R.M.Villoria

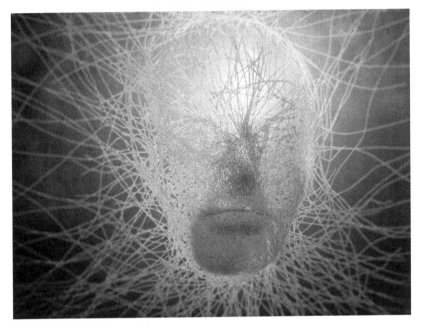

Jason Edwards had always wanted to be a successful artist. As far back as he could ever remember he had always wanted to paint and show people his work. When he was just a child his admiring parents would always have a half a dozen of his "works" either on the refrigerator or taped up somewhere in the house. This validation of his early work only helped to embolden his wishes to not just be a talented artist but an outrageously successful one with a huge following and oodles of money that of course he imagined simply went along with that. But alas as the years went by, poor Jason just couldn't seem to put anything down on canvas that anyone wanted to look at, much less pay real money for. Jason had even gotten himself an agent some years back. They had met at a coffee shop in midtown Manhattan and upon exchanging stories about what each one did, had agreed to a relationship. He wasn't a nationally renowned agent by any stretch of the imagination, however he had promised to show Jason's work wherever he could get him in that might gain Jason some recognition within the artistic community as well as in the public eye.

Year after year passed with closed shows and not so very nice reviews. Jason, now married and living quietly in the Connecticut countryside with his wife Natalie had pretty much resigned himself to the fact that he was basically a failure at his art. Not so much because of the fact that he couldn't seem to paint worth diddely, but more so because he felt his agent wasn't representing him properly. A day didn't pass that his ever so faithful wife didn't encourage him, though she too couldn't help but wonder at times, secretly to herself, if there wasn't perhaps another vocation her dear husband should pursue.

Sitting at the breakfast table one particular morning, she could sense his mood, one of impatience and frustration.

"Darling, why don't you go into the city today?" Natalie offered. "You've been cooped up in that studio for weeks now. You need a change of scenery."

Jason brought his coffee cup down so abruptly he

nearly spilled its contents all over himself. Cursing under his breath at the mishap he pushed back his chair and answered

"Damn it all, he hasn't even called me in almost a month. What does he think I'm doing up here…hibernating?"

"I know sweetheart," Natalie answered trying to offer some comfort. "But you know Andy does have other clients as well to tend to and…"

Braking Natalie off Jason replied;

"Baloney, he's just ignoring me as usual. Does he really think he's gonna retire off that pornographic bullshit Tilton puts out?"

"Well, no honey," Natalie again answered in as reassuring a voice as she could muster. "But he has a lot of shows going on and I'm sure Mr. Tilton is keeping him quite busy."

"What the hell," Jason bellowed. "You think that stuff is good?"

"Why no dear, of course not. Your stuff is much better, I was just suggesting…"

Jason snapped his fingers, pointed and glared at Natalie in a manner she new only to well to mean it was time to say no more, but she did anyway.

"Now, now dear, calm down. Remember what the doctor said."

Now standing at the edge of the table Jason added;

"That sorry assed excuse for a doctor said… (Mimicking a silly voice) *Take the stress out of your life Jason*…Selling my art would go a long way in accomplishing that however it might help just a little if I had an agent that would even bother to call me once in awhile to see what I'm working on."

Jason stormed out of the kitchen and out of the house letting the screen door slam as he did. Natalie knew not to follow him as he was clearly agitated beyond any point where whatever she said to console him would do any good. As she picked up the breakfast dishes she thought, *Real Estate might be nice or maybe a correspondence course in vacuum cleaner repair.*

Midtown was no place to be on a cold and windy autumn day, but as fate would have it Andrew Delaney had to put food on his families table and that meant going into the office on a more regular basis. It seemed that the powers to be had smiled down upon Andy and his fledgling agency recently with the addition of two new clients that had actually begun selling some of their works. Now he was going to have to hire at least one more girl in the office to help him. As he sat across from the next, in what seemed an endless array of applicants who had been washed up from a sea of ineptitude, he wondered if maybe God was playing some cruel joke on him to see how much of this nonsense he could take. The ruse was interrupted suddenly as Gwen, his faithful secretary and confidant, glided into the room with an ever so timely question. She had learned a long time ago that if she ever saw through her bosses office window that he appeared to be either dozing off while listening to some in earnest talent that wanted representation or was nearing a breaking point of throwing a desk accessory across the room, that she should immediately enter his office and rescue him.

"I'm sorry to interrupt you sir, but I was updating the files in the computer and I wondered what category you would like me to place the Edwards file."

This was the one nearly inactive file that was always used for the distraction.

"Do we have a category called ERASE?" he answered raising one eyebrow in hopes that the answer would be affirmative.

Gwen laughed and answered;

"I don't believe so sir."

Turning his attention once again to the starry eyed nymphet sitting across from him he offered his apology.

"I'm sorry but perhaps we could continue our interview

another time? I really must attend to this. I'll tell you what, I'll have my secretary call you," he said gesturing to Gwen to take this person out of his office.

He felt fairly confident that he probably would not be seeing this person again.

Gwen escorted the young woman out into the front office. Andy watched as the applicant left. Andy came out of his office once he knew the coast was clear and walking over to Gwen he leaned down and gave her a quick peck on the cheek saying;

"I can always count on you."

"Yes you can, but you know what?" she answered, "You really do need to do something about this Edwards account. It's been quiet for way to long now."

Andy knew she was right and he also knew exactly what he would have to do though he didn't relish the idea.

"Guess I'm taking a ride out to the country," he said to Gwen I'll be back later today.

As he drove along the turnpike leaving the city, Andy thought about how he dreaded the idea of having this talk with Jason. Knowing how this client's reactions often times were, he imagined what it must be like for a doctor to have to tell a family that their loved one had passed. But the time had finally come.

He remembered their first chance meeting and how excited they both were. Andy had only just opened his agency three months earlier and was eager to pick up new talent and Jason at the prospect of having a professional agent to represent him. Although Andy had embellished considerably about what his entire new agency could offer, he believed that in a matter of time, most of it would be true. Right now though as he drove he wondered just how much time "a matter of time" was exactly.

As he sped along he reflected back on the now several

years he had spent trying to develop this client. Although he had high hopes for this yet undiscovered artist, he was eternally grateful to whomever it was that one is eternally grateful to, that he had developed other clients in time so that he wouldn't be limited to a SPAM diet. He had in fact actually achieved a small measure of success in his industry. Unfortunately over the years it hadn't been as a result of any of the efforts of the man he was on his way to face for the very last time. Although they had had so many discussions on how Jason might develop his craft to be more suitable to an audience, it always seemed to come back to the same thing. Jason believing that it was Andy who had failed him as an agent. But now with several new clients in the wings and a number of revenue producing clients already in place, Andy really couldn't spend any more time nurturing this artist who for all intents and purposes probably would never make it. As the city disappeared behind him, Andy felt content that he was making the right decision to sever their affiliation at this time.

Fall was always so beautiful in Connecticut. Jason always felt indebted to his wife for talking him into moving out of the city where the air seemed so much clearer and cleaner. She had hoped that the change would inspire him to produce great works. Now, five years later, as he stood in their back yard, he still was stuck in the same old rut. How many meadows can a man paint in a lifetime he wondered? There seemed to be an endless amount of them stacking up in the attic. Jason dismissed the thought with a shrug and fanned the large heavy canvas tarp out onto the lawn. Smelling the burning leaves in the neighborhood, he was inspired to work outdoors today. Perhaps being out in the crisp autumn air would help clear his brain and he would be able to create a masterpiece later on. Smiling at the foolishness of that thought, he pulled the Toro chipper/vac out of the shed and onto the lawn. Now this was an inspired piece of work he thought One piece of machinery that could do so many things. Sheer genius. Chip all the dead branches that had fallen creating great mulch for his wife's garden. Vacuum up all the leaves that were constantly falling for months, yes this was easy work and he enjoyed it.

As he began chopping the branches off the overgrown bushes near the garage and feeding them into the chipper, the drone of the engine caused him to drift off in thought back to a conversation he had with his then new agent.

"So you actually think I'll be able to have my own showing in a gallery one day?" he had asked.

"Certainly," Andy had said. "And with my managing techniques it won't be too long before your name will be right up there with Wyeth and oh...what's that other guy's name?"

Although it had only been their first meeting at Andy's office, Jason put all his trust in this man who sat before him. He remembered picking up the business card off the table and reading it.

Andrew Dehaney,
TALENTED ARTISTS MANAGEMENT INTERNATIONAL

It looked all so professional he had thought. But as the years went by, Jason began losing faith in this rather short and smooth talking agent he had contracted with. It seemed to Jason that Andy just wasn't trying very hard. His paintings were good he thought, good as anything else he'd seen. Even his wife had always told him; "Honey, your work is as good as anything I've ever seen." He believed her and he believed in his landscapes. Now he thought, he would just have to make his agent realize just how good his work was. As he threw a particularly thick branch into the chipper he felt a tugging on his shirtsleeve.

"Oh my God!" he screamed as he spun around.

Standing there tugging on his sleeve was Natalie with that wonderfully dazed smile she regularly had on her face when she would talk with him.

"You scared the shit out of me," he yelled over the sound of the chipper. "I thought I'd caught my sleeve on the machine!"

Jason pushed the stop button on the chipper and the drone of the machine slowly came to a halt.

"I'm sorry honey, I didn't mean to scare you," Natalie responded. "I just came out to tell you that Andy just called. He wanted to make sure you were here. He called from his car and said he'd be here in about 30 minutes."

"Did he say what he wanted? Does he have a showing for me?" Jason asked anxiously.

"I'm sorry honey, he didn't say. Shall I make some lemonade?" Natalie asked.

"Sure, sure, you go ahead," Jason answered,

As Natalie turned and walked back towards the house, Jason pushed the on button and the machine began it's load drone again.

I have to think. What pieces should I show? I wonder where the showing will be? He wondered.

As Jason continued feeding branches into the chipper he began daydreaming. He imagined himself at a high-end gallery in New York signing autographs and sipping champagne. With his imagination running rampant, he lost track of time and he didn't see that the bag catching the wood chips was filled to almost bursting. With the next branch, it suddenly popped off the chute and fell to the ground. The next piece of limb Jason had fed into the machine sent wood chips flying out of the chute and onto the tarp lying on the lawn. Jason laughed as he was suddenly brought back to reality and reached down and picked up the fallen bag.

Leaving the machine running, Jason walked around the house and dumped the bag of chips where Natalie could use them around her roses. As he returned to the chipper, he saw Andy's silver BMW round the curve at the corner of the property. Andy hadn't been out to their house in over a year so Jason felt his heart leap just a little in anticipation for what he knew must be exciting news. He didn't want to seem too anxious so he dropped the bag to the ground and started cutting some small branches. Andy pulled in the driveway and honked. Jason turned and waved. As Andy walked towards him, Jason reached over and turned the chipper off. As the drone of the engine subsided, Jason spoke first.

"Long time no see," he said extending his hand in a greeting.

"I know," Andy replied. "It's been way to long since we've seen each other."

"We haven't even talked in over six months," Jason added trying to hold back any trace of sarcasm that might be detected in his voice. After all, he didn't want to seem ungrateful for Andy coming all this way with what he hoped was good news.

"Six months, has it really been that long? How time flies. Well, you know how business is and all," Andy continued.

"No actually I really don't know how business is Andy. Tell me, how's business?" Jason asked still trying not to sound at all perturbed at what he felt was small talk and rather lame small talk at that.

Andy seemed to shuffle a little in his tracks as he continued.

"Well, you know. It's uh...busy. How's everything been for you out here? How's the missus?"

Jason took a deliberate minute to reply. He slowly walked completely around Andy watching him fidget with his car keys. He wondered if Andy had developed a nervous habit from being so busy working.

"Natalie's fine," Jason finally replied. "But you don't look so good Andy. You seem a bit nervous. Are you nervous Andy?"

Andy turned sharply to look straight at Jason.

"No...no, nothing like that, just a lot on my mind, you know," he said.

"Well, you know Andy," Jason began a bit impatiently. "I've had a lot on my mind for months now too. Like when am I going to have another showing or when am I gonna get a call from you with some kind of work, or to even see how I'm doing?"

"Now see....that's....uh exactly what I came out here for," Andy answered. "To talk with you about your work."

"Yeah?" Jason asked.

"Well," Andy continued. "We're getting a lot of activity on some of our artists and you know what that means. I'm flying here and there setting things up and at the same time trying to promote some of our other artists."

"Yeah, and?" Jason asked again.

"Well let's face it Jason," Andy replied. "You know as well as I that it hasn't been easy trying to get your work out there. You haven't done anything different in a very long time and the people I deal with want newer stuff."

"So what are you saying exactly Andy?" Jason asked, his voice beginning to take on an air of exasperation. "Have you got something for me or not, or did you drive all the way out here to tell me nothing?"

"Well...um...not exactly," Andy stammered. "I do have to talk to you about something very important."

Jason was clearly beginning to grow impatient with this game Andy seemed to be playing with him and so he turned his back on Andy and reached for a branch.

"Listen Jason," Andy continued. "You've known me for a long time. You have to understand that there are some decisions that have to be made in business whether we like them or not."

Jason really didn't like the vibes he was getting from this conversation and so he turned abruptly to face Andy. He leaned in closer and clenching his fist said very deliberately;

"Listen you little shithead, I don't really care what decisions you have to make in business, your job is to get me showings and you're not doing your job!"

"Jason, Jason...you don't understand," Andy pleaded.

"NO, YOU DON'T UNDERSTAND!" Jason yelled angrily. "You're supposed to be working for me and I haven't seen squat from you!"

The two men stood staring at each other for several minutes neither one saying a word. Jason being a good foot and a half taller than the diminutive Andy struck a menacing pose. The tension had grown so thick between the two men it seemed almost choking.

Finally, Andy took a step closer and reaching up and placing his hand gently on Jason's shoulder he spoke quietly.

"There's just no easy way to put this Jason. I came out here today to tell you that I can't represent you any longer. It's just not economically sound for me to do. I'm sorry, really I am but sooner or later you're going to have to accept the fact that your work... is just not commercially acceptable."

Jason felt the rage rise up from his belly through his chest and shoulders and into his head. It suddenly felt as if his head would burst with anger. He shoved Andy's hand off his shoulder and turned away.

"Look," Andy said. "We've known each other for a long time Jason. There's no reason why we can't still be friends."

Suddenly Jason turned and grabbing Andy's collar he literally lifted him up off the ground and brought his face right up to his own. His words were strong and deliberate.

"Listen you lousy little son of a bitch, I'm gonna sue you for everything you've got. I'll sue you for mismanagement or misrepresentation or breach of contract, I don't know, but I'm gonna get you!"

Jason threw him down and watched as he fell to the ground on his back.

Andy knew that this wasn't going to be pleasant but he hadn't expected to be roughed up like this and now he was getting a little angry himself.

"What's the matter with you!" he yelled at Jason. "Are you crazy or something? Can't you figure it out on your own? Your work stinks! Nobody wants it! Nobody wants you!"

Jason was through listening to what now was just noise coming out of Andy's mouth. He ignored Andy and to drown him out, turned on the chipper. Andy had gotten up and was now even louder as he hurled insult after insult at Jason trying to get in his face.

"...and furthermore if you ever come near my office, I'll have you arrested. You couldn't paint a chair! I don't know why you ever thought you could...you..."

Jason had all that he could take and in one swift move turned and picked Andy up off the ground and threw him.

The sound was horrifying. It was over in an instant. Everything seemed to go in slow motion from the moment Jason saw the heel of Andy's shoe disappear into the mouth of the chipper. There was blood. So much of it and tiny fragments of bone, flesh and muscle spewed out into the air. Most all of the remains landed on the canvas tarp spread out on the lawn before him as the motor choked to a standstill. Everything suddenly seemed so quiet. He wasn't sure if he was in shock or what, but he carefully folded up the tarp and it's grotesque contents within and pulled it into the garage. Jason walked out to the driveway, got into Andy's car and drove away. Later, as he walked into the kitchen he said nothing as he poured himself a glass of lemonade.

"Where did you guys go? Is Andy coming in for some lemonade?" Natalie asked in her usually upbeat tone.

"No, he had to leave suddenly," Jason quietly answered.

That night Jason sat for hours in the garage just staring at the tarp.

A showing at the Forrest Gallery in New York City is probably one of thee richest rewards any artist can hope for in their career and certainly Jason Edwards could not have ever imagined that he would be here and yet, here he was, standing amidst the news media, surrounded by autograph seekers and fending off queries from some of the country's most prestigious agencies.

A voice called out from the crowd;

"Tell us Mr. Edwards, what do you call this magnificent work you have here?"

Jason glanced over at the wall on which hung the large canvas work.

"I call it...THE AGENT," he answered.

"How irreverent," he heard someone say half laughing.

A small man with glasses stepped up to Jason and tugged lightly on the sleeve of his tuxedo.

"Excuse me sir, but who is representing your work these days?" the man asked.

"I'm in between agents you might say," Jason responded.

"Are you working on anything new?" the man asked. "I think our office would like to talk with you about representation."

"Come out to my home in the country," Jason answered with a wry smile. "We can talk about my next project."

THE END

Tales from the Mind Field

LONG DISTANCE LOVE
By
R.M.Villoria

Chapter One

It was early spring of 1976 and all the things you hope for in a new season were taking place. Gardens were starting to bloom. People who had been kept mostly inside because of the weather were now out and about. Fishing poles and tackle were starting to show up on the shelves of old man Thompson's Hardware store and I had taken up my usual place in front of that store on the porch, relaxing in my favorite wicker rocker that had weathered over some twelve years or so.

Now I've seen a lot of strange things from my vantage point over the years but I guess I'd have to say that when the summer of '76 rolled around I, along with a lot of other folks here in Toreville, witnessed a real different kind of sweet, but strange happening.

I guess it all began one afternoon when that old burgundy '47 Plymouth drove past and turned down Main St. and parked in front of Ms. Gilton's boarding house. Pretty little coupe she was. Obviously someone had put a lot of love into this restoration. Though the tires weren't original, from every angle it appeared as if it had just come off the showroom floor that very day.

The sign in the front window of the boarding house must have caught the eye of the young man that stepped from the car. He disappeared into the foyer of the old house and after about ten minutes reappeared. He went down to his car and gathered a small suitcase and returned to the house no doubt having rented a room from old lady Gilton. Fortunate for her, she still had that old house after her husband died a few years back. Tragic thing him dying like that. He never did recover from the loss of their son in Vietnam in '68. Broke his heart.

To make ends meet Agnes Gilton decided she would rent out some of the rooms. It had worked out well for her, as she had no problem keeping rooms rented regularly. Fortunate for this young man, one had come available just last week.

Later that evening at Luke's Diner where several of us old timers would gather and talk about that days events, albeit they were few, Agnes came in late as she often did after her work at the house to have a cup of tea and sit and talk.

"I see you got a new boarder," I offered as she sat down at the counter next to me.

"Yep," she answered. "A real nice young man. He's from somewhere back east I think. He'll be looking for some work Lucas if you have any," Agnes added as Lucas Miller set a coffee and a tea down in front of us.

"I don't know that I need any help right now," Lucas answered. "Maybe he can line something up out at the mill."

Agnes took a sip of her tea and setting it back down on the saucer replied;

"I'll tell him about that. He was asking about work around here. Seems he likes the area and wants to stay a little while."

The Mill as it was known, was down near the end of town and was still cranking out lumber for locals, though most of that work had long since gone off to the big city some 175 miles away. But it kept a few of the local men busy and gainfully employed. How many more years it would last, nobody really knew. As several more of the locals came by, the evening continued with more talk, some gossip and laughter going on till near midnight when Lucus finally kicked us all out.

Next day I was picking up some aspirin at the Rexall when in walked that same young man from yesterday. He walked up and down a few aisles picking up some items and headed for the checkout counter. I watched him as I sat down at the end of the counter. Fountains, as they were called back in my day were disappearing fast from drug stores, but here in our small town we still had the pleasure of ordering up a soda or a coffee or a piece of pie after some shopping.

"Stella, I swear girl you keep getting prettier every year," I said as the young girl behind the counter came up to me.

Stella Bingham was Charlie's seventeen year-old daughter. Every spring after school would let out for summer break, she'd come over here and work the soda fountain.

"Glad its summer vacation again?" I asked as she wiped the counter in front of me.

"You bet Mr. Stevens. What can I get you?" she asked.

"How about a piece of that cherry pie you've got over there and a Coke," I answered.

"Coming right up," she replied and scurried off to fill my order.

As I waited, I saw that the young man had paid for his supplies and was now approaching the counter. He sat down at the other end and took his baseball cap off and placed it and his bag on the stool next to him. Stella looked over at him and said;

"I'll be right with you."

The young man gave her a thumbs up and smiled. As Stella went about getting my pie and soda I couldn't help but notice how the young man didn't take his eyes off her. *Cute,* I thought.

"Here you go Mr. Stevens. Would you like anything else?" she asked as she set my order down in front of me.

"Nope, I'm good," I replied. "You go ahead and take care of your other customer there."

Stella walked down to the other end of the counter and order pad in hand took the young man's request. He too would have a piece of pie and a soda. As Stella went about getting the young man his order, his eyes never left her. He had a nice smile on his face.

I called down to him.

"That's a pretty nice looking car you've got their young man. I saw you drive by yesterday."

He turned his attention to me and replied.

"Thank you sir. Yeah, my dad gave it to me when I graduated High School. He only drove it a couple of years."

"Nice. How do you keep it so clean?" I asked.

"Wipe it down everyday," he answered.

"Very nice."

I went about finishing up my pie and soda. I left a five dollar bill on the counter to cover my order and a generous tip and walked towards the exit. I stopped as I came up to the young man and putting my hand out said;

"I'm Howard Stevens, What's your name?"

"Jimmy, Jimmy Hargrove," he replied as he turned on his stool to shake my hand.

"Well Jimmy, welcome to Toreville," and I walked out of the store. There parked a couple of spaces down was that beautiful car of his. It looked so new you would have thought it had been bought yesterday.

I went by old man Thompson's next to pick up a new pair of grass shears. Foolishly I had left my pair outside this last winter and they were so rusty I couldn't even get them to work. I looked around the garage for some WD-40 but the can was empty.

"Hey John," I called out as I entered the store. "Where you keeping the grass shears?"

"In the back on the left by the feed," he answered.

When I got up to the counter to pay a short line had formed.

"You here alone John?" I asked.

"Yeah, Pete got another job over in Blain. Guess I'll be holding things down here by myself for awhile."

"Any of the kids from school available?" I went on.

"Haven't talked to any but a few and they weren't right for the job," John answered.

As I waited my turn I thought about the young man who had come to town yesterday. Agnes had mentioned last night that he would be looking for work.

"Hey John, there's a young man, his name is Jimmy, just got into town. He's staying over at Agnes's place and I heard he's looking for work. I met him this morning. Seems like a nice young man. Maybe you want to check it out?"

"Well, if you think he might fill the bill, I'll go over there later and talk to him. Thanks," John said.

I walked out of the store thinking to myself that maybe I had just done my good deed for the day. I opened the door on my old pickup and looking up the street at the Rexall, I noticed that young man's car still parked out front. I smiled as I thought to myself, *maybe the two of them are getting to know each other.*

It rained that night, one of those light spring rainfalls that promised fresh flowers and clean air tomorrow.

Stella woke early and hurried through her chores so as not to be late for her job at the fountain. A slight thrill ran through her this morning. She wondered if that nice boy she'd talked with yesterday at work might come in again today. As she walked into the kitchen for breakfast, she bid her Mom a cheery, "Good morning" as she reached in the fridge for the orange juice.

"Well, you're bright and cheery this morning little lady," her mom said.

"Yep," Stella replied as she poured her little sister and herself a glass of juice and sat down at the table.

Stella's mom noticed her daughter's unusually upbeat mood and inquired;

"So why so cheery today honey? You're usually not all that excited about working on Saturday."

"Oh, it's nothing," she replied and giggled a bit.

After breakfast, Stella helped her mom put the dishes in the sink and with a quick kiss on her cheek said goodbye to her mom and ran out to her bike. She felt like her bicycle was flying as she made her way into town and up to the Rexall. As she approached the store her heart seemed to skip a beat and she actually felt herself get flushed. There was the young man's car parked right in front of the store. She locked the bike to the bicycle rack in front and entered. She immediately saw Jimmy seated at the counter. He turned and smiled.

"Hi," he said as she walked behind the counter and grabbed the apron she always wore.

"Hi yourself," she answered not trying to show just how happy she was that he was there.

"Guess what, I think I got a job down the street at the hardware store. The owner came by the boarding house where I'm staying and talked with me about it for over an hour yesterday. I'm supposed to go by and see him in about fifteen minutes."

"Wow, that's great," Stella answered still trying hard not to show just how excited she was now that the prospect of him staying there in Toreville longer existed.

"You want a soda before you go?" she asked.

"Thanks," Jimmy replied.

Stella leaned on her elbows on the counter for the next ten minutes' listening to whatever the dreamy young man in front of her was saying. She really didn't care. She only knew that he was so cute and so much more mature than all the boys she had gone to school with here. She imagined spending a lot of time with him.

"Well, I guess I'd better get up there," Jimmy added as he stood up to leave. Stella jumped up as though suddenly awakened from a dream.

"Oh, yeah," she blurted out. "I guess so. Let me know if

- 200 -

you get the job okay?"

"Okay," he said as he started for the door he turned and asked; "Are you doing anything tonight? You must have a movie theatre here in town right? You want to go?"

Stella seemed to stutter as she answered.

"Uh, yes, I mean yes. I mean yes we have a theatre."

"Well? You wanna go with me?" Jimmy asked.

There was no hesitation in Stella's excited reply.

"YES!"

Jimmy turned and ran out to his car and drove down to the hardware store. He thought as he drove that this might just be the best day of his life.

Into the Rexall walked Stella's two closest friends and they had a seat.

"What is wrong with you Stell?" the young girls chimed as they sat at the fountain. "I wanted a chocolate soda not cherry and Ginger here asked you for a piece of pie not cake. You got your head up you butt?"

Stella laughed as she picked up the incorrect orders and apologized. She began telling the girls about the boy she had met yesterday. They wanted all the juicy details. There really wasn't that much to tell except that she and he were going to the movies tonight.

"Oh yeah, we'll be there. I've got to see this guy," Ginger said.

JoAnn sitting next to Ginger inquired;

"You really like this guy eh?"

"Oh no silly, I hardly know him," Stella answered as she went down the counter to wait on another person.

The two girls looked at each other and giggled.

"Yep she likes him," they squealed in unison.

Chapter Two

John watched from near the opening of the stock room as Jimmy waited on one after another of his customers with real professionalism and manners. Since he started him immediately this morning he hadn't been disappointed in anything Jimmy had done so far. In fact he was thinking that he was kind of glad Pete had decided to go over to Blain for work. This kid was like having two Pete's.

"I like your new help," a voice spoke from nearby.

It was Ms. Highton, a woman who came in the store at least twice a week for something. Odd too, John thought since she wasn't married and never did any work around her condo.

"Thanks," he answered. "I think he's gonna work out just fine."

"Alright young man," John spoke as Jimmy finished up with the last customer of the day. "I'm real pleased with your work so I'll see you back here Monday morning okay?"

"Thank you Mr. Thompson, but aren't you open on Sundays?" Jimmy asked.

"Yes but I can handle it. It's usually pretty slow on Sunday. You go on and enjoy the rest of your weekend."

"Thank you again for the job," Jimmy answered as he walked out the front door.

"Your welcome son," John called after him.

As Jimmy tied the lace on his shoe he thought how lucky he was that after only a few days in town he had already gotten a job and a date with what he thought was probably the most beautiful girl in town. He headed out to his car to go pick up Stella. He grabbed a cloth he had on the seat and began wiping down the dashboard. He always wanted the car to look as clean as possible.

As he drove, he looked down at the gauge. *Darn,* he thought. *Need some gas.* He pulled into the station at the corner and stopped in front of the pump. He waited for a moment to see if he would have to pump the gas himself when a man walked up to his window and asked.

"Fill er' up?"

"Sure, thanks," he answered.

As he sat waiting, the attendant called out to him.

"Really nice restoration you have here."

Jimmy looked back at him and answered;

"Oh no, it's all original. Nothing's been done to it."

"Wow," the attendant called back. "You keep it in really good shape."

"Yeah my dad did too," Jimmy responded.

"That'll be eight fifty. You were almost empty," the attendant said as he stepped up to the window.

Jimmy sat there for a moment, *Boy; things are really expensive in this town. That's gonna cut into my money for tonight with Stella* he thought. He reached into his back pocket and pulled a ten-dollar bill out of his billfold.

"Keep the change," Jimmy told him as he started up the Plymouth. Although he was now about six dollars shorter than he thought he'd be, his father had always told him to be generous with people who serve you in any capacity. It would always pay off in the long run.

"Thanks," the attendant yelled after him as he pulled away.

He and Stella had agreed to meet in front of the Rexall that evening and would walk the two blocks to the theatre.

When he pulled up she was already waiting there. He felt bad and hoped that she hadn't been waiting long.

"I'm sorry," he said as he got out of the car. "I had to stop and get gas."

"That's okay," Stella answered.

She was just so happy that he showed up. Her girlfriends were taking bets that he might not. After all, "You don't even know him" they were saying.

The two walked together down Main Street the two blocks to the theatre talking about Jimmy's new job and Stella's experiences behind the fountain each day. They laughed as comfortably as though they had known each other for far longer than the few days that had passed. Stella wanted to know all about where Jimmy had come from but he really didn't want to talk too much about that. Instead he was more interested in learning all he could about her. Stella explained that between school and her job at the fountain, life was really not terribly exciting around Toreville.

As they approached the theatre, a small group of boys rushed past them. One of the boys yelled out;

"Hey Stella, don't hang out with strangers!" The boys laughed as they passed and ran into the theatre entrance.

Standing out front were Ginger, JoAnn and two other of Stella's friends from school.

"Uh oh, I think we're going to get ambushed here," she said apologetically as they approached the girls.

Jimmy chuckled as though he understood what was going on.

"Oh Hi Stell, are you going to the movies too?" they asked even though they all had advance notice of Stella's date tonight with the new boy in town.

"You guys," Stella responded sarcastically.

They all walked up to the ticket booth. Stella's friends fell back a little and whispering and giggling, they let Stella and Jimmy get their tickets first.

"Two please," Jimmy offered.

"That'll be four dollars," the young girl in the booth said.

Jimmy reached for his billfold again and took out a five dollar bill. The look on his face must have concerned Stella because she asked;

"Is that okay? I know you just started your job and all. We don't have to go if you want."

"No, no it's okay. Just seemed a bit high."

"What did you use to pay where you lived?" Stella asked.

"A **lot** less," Jimmy replied.

They took the tickets and went inside.

Aside from a little giggling and whispers from Stella's friends seated a few rows back, they enjoyed the movie and upon leaving decided it would be nice to go get a soda.

"Can we not go over to the Rexall?" Stella asked.

Jimmy understood that after working there everyday, Stella probably would rather have a change of scenery.

"Where to?" he asked.

"Well, across the bridge is a coffee shop and sometimes we go there for fries and shakes on the weekends," Stella offered.

They drove the two miles to the coffee shop Stella had wanted to go to and once there, they stayed for hours just talking, laughing and getting to know each other better.

"Do you know what time it is?" Stella's mother said as Stella bounded up the front porch steps.

"Oh Mom, you scared me. I didn't see you sitting there," Stella answered half out of breath from running after Jimmy had dropped her off at the end of the drive.

"You're father has already gone to bed so be quiet. Come sit here with me," Stella's mom said as she gestured for Stella to take a seat next to her on the porch swing.

"Who was that boy that dropped you off?" she asked. "I've never seen that car before," she added.

"Oh Mom, he's so wonderful. He just moved to town last week and he works at the hardware store and..." Stella's Mom cut her off.

"And he keeps you out this late?" she asked.

"I'm sorry mother. We were just over at Denny's talking and talking and well, the time just got away from us."

"Where is this boy from? Is he from around here? What's his name?" Mom asked.

"His name's Jimmy and no, he's not from here," Stella replied. "Someplace back east I think, I'm not sure."

Stella wanted to share even more of her excitement about Jimmy with her mother but her mom cut her off again.

"Well young lady, I think you had better go on upstairs and get some sleep. You have church in the morning."

Stella leaned over and gave her mother a kiss on the cheek, then jumped up and hurried off into the house. Stella's Mom remained sitting on the porch for a while contemplating this apparent infatuation her daughter had with this unknown new boy.

The next morning at breakfast, Stella's father looked up from his paper and asked her;

"I understand from your mother that you got in here pretty late last night. Around twelve thirty was it?"

"Yes," Stella answered. "I'm sorry daddy, it won't happen again."

"I think we ought to meet this boy. Why don't you invite him over after church this morning," he went on.

"I don't know if he goes to church," Stella answered.

"Oh," was all her father said.

"Well I think he must have come by here early before sunrise and dropped your bike off by the porch," Stella's mom chimed in.

"Really?" Stella asked, thinking that she wished she had been awake so she could have seen him.

All through church that morning Stella could hardly sit still. She fidgeted in her pew and wanted the service to be over as fast as possible so that she could go see Jimmy. When they all got home she ran upstairs and changed quickly. Half running through the kitchen to the front door Stella called out,

"I'm going to go see if Jimmy will come over so you guys can meet him."

As the front screen door slammed, Stella's mom called after her;

"Don't be long."

Stella's younger sister asked her mom;

"Who's Jimmy?"

"Just a boy your sister met," Mom answered, "Just a boy."

Stella flew into town on her bike and headed over to Ms. Gilton's boarding house. She jumped off her bike letting it fall to the ground and ran up the three steps to the porch. Agnes Gilton was kneeling down in the garden by the front porch as Stella ran past her.

"He's not here," she called up to Stella just as she was about to open the screen door.

Stella turned and asked;

"Do you know where he is?"

Although only days had passed since these two kids had met, between the girls in town gossiping and their parents overhearing it, Agnes had already heard that there seemed to be something going on with these two.

"No, he left fairly early this morning and I haven't seen

him since," Agnes added.

Turning with a look on her face as if a puppy had died, Stella slowly walked off the porch. Agnes watched as she picked up her bike and began to walk it down the drive.

"Shall I tell him you were here?" she called after Stella.

"Thanks," Stella called back.

Stella rode around town for over an hour looking to see if she could find Jimmy anywhere but without success. She came across Ginger and JoAnn and asked them if they had seen him but they too had not. The three girls sat down on the grass at the park in the center of town and Stella shared how she was beginning to feel about this boy.

"I don't know what it is about him but I'm crazy about him," Stella said.

"Well, he is cute and he has a pretty cool car," JoAnn offered.

"What do your parents think of him?" Ginger asked.

"I was going to introduce him to them today. That's why I'm looking for him," Stella answered.

"Well, don't worry. He probably just went over to Blain or something," JoAnn added.

"You should probably slow down a little Stell," Ginger warned. "You really don't know him all that well yet."

Stella nodded her head and answered.

"Yeah well, tell that to my heart."

JoAnn whistled and said;

"Boy you've got it bad girl."

The three of them laughed and decided to go on over to the fountain for a soda.

Chapter Three

The next day was a busy one at the Rexall, lots of folks filling prescriptions and just shopping for things in general. The fountain was also busy most of the morning with moms and their kids, Stella's friends and now the lunch hour was just about on them. Stella had already heard from her friends that Jimmy was at work at the hardware store so she felt good that he was around. About one o'clock, he walked in. All the seats at the fountain were still taken so he walked back and forth following Stella as she waited on her customers. She was so excited to see him and it showed. Several of the people at the counter looked back and forth at the two of them and smiled. Finally a stool came available and in a flash Jimmy sat down.

"I'm glad you're here," Stella said as she picked up the dirty dishes in front of him.

Jimmy beamed and answered;

"So am I."

"Where were you yesterday?" she asked.

"Took the car out for a good long run. Helps to keep the engine clean," he answered.

"You really love that car don't you?" Stella said.

"More than anything, well, not more than ANYTHING anymore," he said smiling.

Stella blushed knowing exactly what he meant and wiped the counter in front of him. She hesitated for a moment and then began to mouth "I, I lo...." But decided that might not be a good idea even though she was beginning to feel it. She blew him a kiss and went to continue her work.

Jimmy smiled and winked.

The rest of that summer was magical for Stella. Her parents had met Jimmy and really liked him. She and he did everything together. Her friends all liked him as well and many times they would all get together and picnic or go to the movies. Some of the boys from school even wanted him to come out and play baseball with them and talked about how they would all get together and watch the World Series at the end of the season but Jimmy spent every waking moment with Stella. He did however, tell them that the Yankees were gonna beat the Dodgers. They all laughed and chided him saying;
"Yeah, if they even play."
Each Sunday afternoon, Stella would help him wash the Plymouth. He kept it spotless as much as possible. He would tell her how he never wanted to see a single scratch on it anywhere. She would kid him when he would go out to it after a rainfall and wipe it down. He would tell her how it was his father's pride and joy and how it helped him remember him. Although he spoke of his father whenever he spoke about the car, Jimmy was never forthcoming when it came to his own family. That bothered Stella often and she told him so but he would always manage to change the subject.

There were many more nights that Stella got home later than her parents were happy with, but they had agreed between them that their daughter seemed to be in good hands so they let it slide, but not without a few gentle reminders. One night in particular around mid-summer when they had parked well out of town in what had now become their favorite retreat across the road from the old junkyard and were talking about what they wanted to do with their lives, Stella stopped suddenly mid sentence and took Jimmy's hand.

"Do you love me?" she asked.

"Of course I do. You know I do," he insisted.

"Next year I'm going to graduate. I don't know if I want to go on to college or not," she said. "My parents want me to but..."

"You have to," Jimmy answered assertively. "You're smart. You can do terrific things with your life."

"If I went away would you go with me?" she asked tentatively.

Jimmy was silent for a long time.

"I don't know," he finally offered. "I'm happy here and I don't know where I will end up from one day to the next."

"If you're happy here, why would you end up anywhere else?" Stella asked quizzically.

Jimmy just stared straight out the windshield and didn't answer. They sat there in silence these two love struck young people not knowing what the future held for them. Eventually, Stella fell asleep on Jimmy's shoulder while he continued to be lost in a trance staring out at the night. The sight of the flashlight in the rear view mirror broke Jimmy's stare. He quickly glanced at his watch. 3:23 a.m. All he could think of was how angry Stella's parents were gonna be. He nudged her awake as a sheriff's deputy came up to his side window.

"What are you kids doing out here at this hour?" he asked Jimmy through the open window,

"I'm sorry sir. We just sort of lost track of time," Jimmy answered.

"Well, I'd suggest you get her home since her parents have been calling our office now for about the last two hours," the deputy said.

"Yes Sir," Jimmy answered as he started up his car and turned on the headlights. Stella reached up and kissed him gently on the cheek.

"I'm gonna be in so much trouble with your parents," Jimmy said worriedly as he turned the car up on to the road and headed back towards town.

"It'll be okay," Stella whispered in his ear. As she

- 211 -

glanced over at the graveyard of old rusted automobiles, she hoped she was right.

As they drove up Stella's driveway, the porch light shone through the darkness. Stella's father came through the front door and out onto the porch. They both jumped out of the car and ran up on to the porch.

"I'm so, so sorry sir, it was all my...." but before he could finish his sentence, Stella's dad put his arm around his daughter's shoulder and turning to go inside said over his shoulder;

"We'll talk about this another day son," and went inside.

The porch light went out and Jimmy's heart sank. Had he ruined a perfectly good thing here? Would he be allowed to see Stella again? He left the porch and drove home to his room at the boarding house.

The next day Jimmy went right over to the Rexall to see Stella but she wasn't there. He sat at the counter for an hour but still she didn't come. Worried, he left and drove out to her house. He figured he might as well face whatever her father had in store for him sooner than later. As he knocked on the door his heart jumped as he saw Stella through the sheer curtain on the door walking to answer it.

"Hi sweetie," she answered in a surprisingly upbeat tone. "I just woke up twenty minutes ago. I called down to the store to let them know I wouldn't be there 'till later. They said I didn't have to come in today if I didn't want to, I don't know. Maybe I will. Come on in the kitchen."

Jimmy followed her into the kitchen surprised that there wasn't a more gloomy feeling in the air here considering their late night last evening.

"Is everything okay?" he whispered as Stella took his

hand and walked through the swinging door into the bright kitchen.

There was Stella's mother fixing pancakes at the stove and Stella's little sister sitting at the table.

"I'm making some breakfast for our late riser here Jimmy, would you like some?" Stella's mom asked.

"Uh…okay," he answered tentatively.

He glanced over at Stella as he sat down with a look to ask again if everything was okay.

"You kids sure gave us a scare last night," her mother said as she placed a plate of pancakes down in the center of the table. "You should have at least called us son if you thought you were going to be at all late."

"I'm so sorry Ms. Bingham. The time just slipped away from me and Stell and well, I guess I really don't have a good excuse," Jimmy offered as he took a few pancakes onto the plate Stella had placed in front of him. Stella's little sister giggled and Stella's mom just smiled and said;

"Well, like Stella's father told her this morning, don't **EVER** let it happen again."

Again? Jimmy thought. There would be more time together for them. His worst fears were unrealized. His shoulders dropped as he happily reached for the maple syrup. He looked over at Stella who was beaming and smiling from cheek to cheek.

"There's a carnival that comes here every summer," Stella said excitedly. "It starts on Friday. Let's go okay?" she asked Jimmy.

Jimmy looked over at her mother as if for approval.

"Just make sure you get home a lot earlier than last night," Stella's mom admonished.

The rest of the week seemed to take forever waiting for Friday night when the two of them would go to the carnival. Stella worked at the fountain and Jimmy came by each day during his lunch hour.

When Friday finally arrived the small town seemed all a buzz over the upcoming highlight of the summer. Jimmy heard almost everyone talking about it at the hardware store and Stella served several of the carnival employee's lunch both Thursday and Friday as they started setting up.

"Why don't you go ahead and finish up for the day Jimmy," Mr. Thompson said as he stepped in behind the counter where Jimmy was helping a customer.

"Really?" Jimmy asked.

"Sure, you go on ahead."

Jimmy took the cloth from in the trunk and began wiping down the hood on the Plymouth. He painstakingly rubbed each section of the car to insure that it shone as cleanly as possible. He then took the compound he used to polish up the wheel covers and placing a small dab on the cloth carefully rubbed it over the covers leaving a slight film, which he would buff out after a few minutes.

"Aren't you going to the Carnival?" a voice called out as he worked diligently on his prized automobile. It was Agnes as she came down the walk from the house.

"Yes Ma'am, as soon as I'm done here," Jimmy replied standing up as she approached.

He's always such a polite young man. Agnes thought. *Too bad more young people today aren't that way. Yep, there used to be a time.*

Jimmy knelt back down and finished cleaning the last wheel cover. He stood back and surveyed his work. Surely there wasn't another car in the county that looked this good he thought.

As he drove up Stella's drive he saw her come

bounding off the porch to meet him. How could he have gotten so lucky he thought, to have found so beautiful a girl who was so in love with him? A momentary pang of sadness swept over him but upon Stella opening the door to the car it was quickly washed away.

"I want to ride all the rides this year," she exclaimed excitedly as she slipped into the car. "Will you ride them all with me?"

Jimmy nodded his affirmation and they drove off to where the carnival was set up near the end of town.

Stella's friends were already there and ran up to the two of them as they got out of the car. JoAnn slipped up onto the front fender of Jimmy's car squealing;

"Let me take a picture of the two of you!"

As she pulled her Polaroid SX-70 up to her eye Jimmy yelled out.

"Off the car please!"

Stella pulled on JoAnn's arm and slid her off the car onto the parking lot pavement.

"Yeah, nobody sits on Jimmy's car okay?" Stella said for all her friends to hear. "That's a real pet peeve of his," she added, looking back at Jimmy for a note of appreciation.

"Geez, I'm sorry. I just wanted to take your picture," JoAnn said.

"It's okay," Jimmy said quietly as he took the tail of his shirt and wiped the fender where JoAnn had sat.

Stepping back to make sure the fender was clean, he turned and putting his arm around Stella called out to JoAnn;

"Okay, take a picture."

But JoAnn and the others had already begun walking towards the entrance to the carnival. Stella looked up at Jimmy, shrugged her shoulders and smiled.

"Let's go," she said and they too walked towards the entrance.

Two stuffed bears and a frog were the tally so far as the two lovers walked up to the Ferris wheel. Two of her other friends had already gotten on board as they stepped into the seat and pulled the bar down on their laps. Slowly the Ferris wheel began to move forward. Around and around it continued for several minutes.

Down on the ground Ginger turned to JoAnn and said;

"How many pictures do you have left?"

JoAnn looked at the camera and answered;   "Darn, I only have one left."

"Take one of Stella and Jimmy," Ginger shrieked excitedly. "You haven't taken any of them all night."

"Well, he wasn't very nice yelling at me like that earlier," JoAnn answered.

"Oh come on," Ginger replied. "He loves that old car and just doesn't want any scratches on it. Come on, take their picture while they're up there."

Reluctantly, JoAnn raised the camera and clicked off a shot just as they were rounding the crest at the top.

As JoAnn pulled the print from the camera, she uttered;

"What the...where the heck is he? What'd he do drop his head and throw up? He was in the picture when I took it," she yelled over the noise of the machinery.

"Oh come on Jo, you must have moved or something," Ginger replied as the Ferris wheel began to slow to a stop letting the passengers of each car exit.

JoAnn looked at her camera from all angles as if to see a defect or some possible explanation for her missing that shot.

"What did you do up there Jimmy?" JoAnn asked as they exited the ride. "Put your head down and throw up or something? I took one last picture of you and Stell and for some reason you're not in the picture."

"Let me see," Stella asked reaching for the picture. She stareed at it for a moment and turning to Jimmy said; "I didn't see you put your head down. Did you?"

"Nah," he replied. "You must have moved your hands or

- 216 -

got bumped when you took it Jo."

The group of them walked on as JoAnn simply nodded her head in wonderment. They all decided they would go to the Denny's and get sodas and ice cream after the carnival.

"That is unless of course you two need to go out to your lovers lane," Ginger chided addressing Stella and Jimmy.

They all laughed, and then all finalized their plans to all did go to the Denny's that night.

July slipped away and August arrived with no decision from Stella what she would do regarding college after next year. She had already applied and been accepted at the University in Boston, but she was torn now between staying here with the boy she so loved and leaving. Jimmy had already made up his mind that he wanted to stay here in Toreville. He loved his job and his boss had made him a manager of sorts by giving him a key and allowing him to open and close sometimes. Stella wanted him to go with her if she did go but understood that he had his mind made up.

It was getting to be a difficult time for the two of them as neither one wanted the other to sacrifice. Stella's parents made it very clear how they felt. She should of course go on to college and if, as they would so often remind her, Jimmy truly was the boy for her, well then he would still be here while she continued her education. Secretly though they hoped that Stella would outgrow what they considered a summer infatuation and hopefully meet a young man away at school.

There were several teary nights out at Stella and Jimmy's favorite place where they would sometimes sit for hours in his car not saying a word but knowing in there hearts what the other one was thinking.

"You know I'm always going to love you don't you?" Stella would say as they would sit out there. Jimmy too would tout his undying love for Stella. One night as they spoke of plans they would love to see consummated one day, Jimmy stopped mid-sentence and reached across Stella opening the glove box door. It fell flat held by the hinge. He reached inside and took out a folded knife. It was shiny and as he brought it back across Stella's lap, she could see the intricate tooling on the handle. With both hands Jimmy opened the knife and silently held it up in front of them. Stella looked into Jimmy's eyes and gestured a kiss at him. Whatever was going to happen next she thought was going to be something that would be theirs for all time.

"Slide over," Jimmy whispered.

Stella moved some towards the other side.

"All the way, to the door," he added in a quiet voice.

Stella slowly slid across the bench seat of the Plymouth till she was against the passenger door. Jimmy began to move across the seat towards her. A slight shiver ran down Stella's spine, as she wasn't completely certain what Jimmy was going to do next.

"What are you doing?" she asked as he slid across the seat until he was pressing against her again.

"You'll see," and without hesitation, he reached down with his left hand, held the glove box door steady and over the next several minutes he carved into the inside surface of the glove box door.

JH loves SB

Tears rolled down Stella's cheeks as she watched him carefully carve each initial. It wasn't until he was finishing up the last of the B that she suddenly called out;

"But this car is your baby! You never want a scratch on it anywhere. What are you doing?"

"Nothing is as important as you Stell," he answered assertively. "Nothing. I love you forever."

Stella slipped her arms around his neck and they kissed for a very long time.

Chapter Four

Several weeks passed and they continued to dodge the one big subject they both knew was looming just ahead. Away from Jimmy one evening, Stella addressed the issue at home.

"I don't want to go!" Stella cried. "I won't go!"

"You have to go Stella," her father argued. "Your tuition is paid and your schedule is already here. And besides, you need to get that education if you plan on amounting to more than a soda jerk here in this town."

"I want to stay here with Jimmy!" she cried out.

Her mother reached over to comfort her but Stella just jumped up off her bed and stormed out of the room. She sat down on the landing of the staircase leading downstairs. She felt her mother's arm slip around her shoulder as she sat down next to her on the landing.

"Sweetheart, it is for your own good. You don't know. He may be gone before the winter comes."

"I know he won't. He loves me and I love him and we want to get married one day."

Understanding the psychology of parenthood even better than her husband, Stella's mom proceeded.

"Look, after a semester if you still feel this way we can all sit down and discuss it again but right now, you have to go ahead with the plans already in progress."

Stella's stiffness subsided a bit when it seemed her mom was more understanding of her feelings than that of her father. Even though he had spoken of Jimmy many times in only the best of terms, he felt that this was simply a summer romance and that she couldn't put off the plans she had already made.

She left for work and rode her bike slowly down to the Rexall. Jimmy would be by on his lunch break. Mr. Thompson now let Jimmy have an hour and a half for lunch since he had been doing such a good job over the summer.

They would talk about what they would do that day after work or as they did more often now, would just drive out to their spot and sit under the tree in the car and hold each other.

Jimmy would always open the glove box so that Stella could see his gesture of love for her.

About a week later, as I sat at the counter at the Rexall, I watched as Stella worked. She continued to look up at the clock and at the front door repeatedly.

"Isn't here yet?" I asked as she refilled my coffee.

"Oh, he'll be along Mr. Stevens. Must have had to work into his lunch hour a bit," Stella replied.

But as the time continued to pass, Stella seemed more concerned with every passing minute. I got up and placing a ten on the counter, I said;

"I'm going down to Thompson's myself right now Stell. I'll check on him."

"Thank you Mr. Stevens," she called out as I left.

Out front I looked down the block but didn't see that shiny Plymouth out in front of Thompson's Hardware as I usually did.

When I entered the store there were five or six people lined up at the counter. I couldn't see him right away but as I got closer to the front counter I recognized John working the register.

"Hey John," I called out. "Where's Jimmy today?"

"Don't know. Didn't show. Maybe sick," John answered as he waited on the next customer.

I wandered around the store a few minutes and left.

That night as Stella finished up her work, her mother walked in and announced that the entire family was going over to her sister's for dinner and she was there to pick up Stella. Stella desperately wanted to go see Jimmy to make sure he was okay but she figured that he probably was out sick today and she would see him tomorrow. She jumped in the car with her mom and they left.

It started raining at about ten that evening and on their way home Stella and her family had occasion to drive by the boarding house where Jimmy was living. She strained to see through the rain in the darkness for Jimmy's car out front but somehow missed it.

The next morning was clear and smelled refreshing after the heavy rain from the night before. Stella figured she would leave a little early so that she could ride her bike by the hardware store and say hi to Jimmy before she went on up to the Rexall. She hurriedly ate the breakfast her mother had prepared and ran out the door. She pedaled so fast her foot came off the pedal five times along the way. As a result, she bruised her ankle on it. When she rounded the corner of Main and headed up to Thompson's, her heart sank as she didn't see Jimmy's impeccable car sitting out front. Well, maybe he parked around the side she thought.

As she ran into the store, she almost knocked Mr. Thompson down as he came out from behind the corner.

"Where's Jimmy?" she asked.

"Exactly," Mr. Thompson replied. "I'd like to know the answer to that as well. This is two days now without a word."

- 221 -

"Really?" Stella asked. "I thought he was out sick."

"I did too," Thompson answered. "So I called over to Agnes' place this morning and she hasn't seen him either."

"What?" Stella replied and turned and ran out of the store.

She jumped on her bike and rode as fast as she could down the street to Agnes Gilton's boarding house. She dropped her bike in a flurry of dust as she raced up the steps and through the front door. Agnes Gilton was standing in the hallway between the kitchen and the foyer when Stella blurted out;

"Where's Jimmy?"

"Good question young lady," Agnes answered. "He appears to have simply disappeared in the night. His room is cleaned up and all his belongings are gone. I tell you, I have no idea where he went."

Stella was so taken aback by this news she didn't know what to say at first. She just stood there for several minutes and then just screamed;

"NO!"

When Stella wasn't laying on her bed sobbing, she was asking everyone she came in contact with over the next few days if they had seen Jimmy or his car.

"Hard to miss his car," she would say.

Sitting around at night at Luke's Diner, it seemed to be the talk of the town. Everybody was asking how or even more importantly, why this nice young man who was clearly smitten with one of the cutest girls in town just suddenly up and vanished with no notice or reason.

Stella's girlfriends all knew how much she loved Jimmy and had heard all about how they talked about their future and how he had even proclaimed his love by doing what seemed the unthinkable early in their relationship and defacing that beautiful car he kept so immaculate by carving his and her initials into the glove box door.

Two weeks passed and then three, as Ginger and JoAnn stayed close by Stella's side consoling her. The pain, it seemed to Stella, was too much to bear at times and she had even talked about taking her life. They tried so hard to convince her that he had really and truly loved her and that maybe it was just family matters that had taken him away so abruptly. Stella, Ginger and JoAnn drove out to their "favorite" place three times because Stella wanted to "feel" him with her.

Tomorrow would be six months since they had met and Stella wanted to remember him once again at the one spot where they had spent so many nights together, their favorite place across from the old junkyard. The friends agreed to meet that afternoon around three since both Ginger and JoAnn had plans that night.

As they drove out to the spot, Stella talked incessantly about the plans she and Jimmy had made and how he had always told her he would love her for all time.

They pulled in under the trees where she and Jimmy had always parked. They talked for several hours until it appeared the sun was beginning to wane. Ginger started up the car and turned it around to leave when Stella suddenly called out;

"Stop!, Stop the car!"

Ginger hit the brake hard as all three girls nearly slipped off the front seat.

"What? What is it?" JoAnn asked.

Pointing out the front window across a short distance

and into the junkyard Stella called out;

"That's his car! That's Jimmy's car!"

"Stella, your nuts, those cars have been there forever."

"Let me out, let me out!" Stella screamed as she reached over JoAnn and opened the door.

Nearly pushing her girlfriend out on to the ground, Stella jumped out and ran across the road to the chain link fence where the junkyard began. Her girlfriends caught up with her as she turned and running along the length of the fence reached the entrance. There was an old man standing there in overalls by the small wooden building. It had a sign on it that read; OFFICE.

"Is this your junkyard?" Stella asked.

"Yeah, and I'm getting ready to close so you girls scoot. There's no playing around out here," he muttered.

"I have to go in there!" Stella proclaimed.

"Stell, the guy said he's closing," Ginger offered from behind her.

"I don't care," as she pushed past the old man and ran inside the junkyard.

Following suit, her girlfriends did the same and followed Stella as she ran around the maze of dilapidated vehicles that looked like they had been there forever.

Suddenly she came around a partially wrecked pick up truck and stopped cold in her tracks. There just inside the chain link fence along the road before her was a '47 Plymouth.

It did look a lot like Jimmy's car except that this car clearly had been here for at least 20 or 30 years. It was simply a rust bucket. The doors were missing; the roof looked as though the car had been rolled over. There was no glass except the back window and the tires were flat, rotted and worn. The interior was completely torn and even the front bench seat had little or no fabric left on it. As Stella stood there frozen, a rat crawled out from under the front seat and ran away.

"Stella, you don't want to go near that thing," JoAnn admonished. By now the old man had caught up with the girls and was fussing about calling the Sheriff if they didn't get off his property. Ginger turned to him and quieting him down assured him that they would be leaving in a moment.

Stella walked slowly closer to the old beat up car. She circled it, looking it over carefully until she was on the passenger side.

There was no door and the debris inside on the floor was disgusting. Nevertheless, she proceeded closer. The similarity to Jimmy's car was eerie she thought, yet it made her feel a closeness to him that she hadn't been able to feel for weeks now. She cautiously stepped up to the open doorway and slipped into the partially covered seat. The car shifted and several pieces seemed to fall off the car as it did.

With the shift in the vehicle, one of those things that fell was the glove box door. It fell open. Stella let out a gasp and then she slowly began to sob as her girlfriends moved in closer to console her.

What they all saw was not only unexpected, but also actually a little frightening. There etched into the inside of the glove box drawer were the initials;

JH loves SB

But how could that be.

"How long has this car been here?" Ginger turned and asked the old man.

"I don't know. It was here when I bought the yard back in '55 the old man answered.

Stella reached forward and touching the carved letters, she continued sobbing.

THE END

55817394R00142

Made in the USA
Charleston, SC
06 May 2016